Domme Chronicles

Erotic tales of love, passion, & domination

Sharyn Ferns

Copyright © 2013 Sharyn Ferns
All Rights Reserved

No part of this publication may be reproduced, distributed or transmitted in any form or by any means, including photocopying, recording, or other electronic or mechanical methods, without the prior written permission of the publisher, except in the case of brief quotations embodied in critical reviews and certain other non-commercial uses permitted by copyright law.

Domme Chronicles: Erotic tales of love, passion, & domination / Sharyn Ferns -- 1st ed.
ISBN: 1494737051
ISBN-13: 978-1494737054

http://www.domme-chronicles.com

To the incredible men who have graced my life with their submission.

This is for you.

TABLE OF CONTENTS

Introduction i
List of Stories 449
About the Author 457

Introduction

This is a very personal book: A collection of hot intimate memories placed on the page with love and passion, and an incredible desire for more of the same.

Most of it is true. And in that truth is a version of a D/s relationship between a dominant woman and her submissive man that exists in similar forms for many people, but that we don't see so much because it's overwhelmed in the public spaces by the cartoonish stereotypes that misrepresent and devalue both dominant women and submissive men in equal measure.

My sexuality is tied inextricably to my dominance, and that manifests as a fierce and passionate hunger that burns like an endless vortex of energy. When I desire a man, I want everything from him—I want to control, explore, expose, cherish and own him.

I aim those desires at the amazing submissive men who willingly give themselves to me for our mutual pleasure.

Together we make this incredibly intimate connection in our dance of aggression and vulnerability. It's hot and sweet and loving and violent and affectionate and intense and tender, and did I mention insanely fucking hot?

This anthology of erotic vignettes lays bare that passion from my very personal perspective as a dominant woman who is privileged to have known the beautiful submissive men who have become part of my story.

I hope you enjoy it.

Sharyn Ferns
Dec 2013

Note: *All activities described in this book were carried out with the enthusiastic consent of the parties involved, and with the safety risks assessed. No submissives were harmed in the making of these memories.*

Biting him

She beckoned him onto the bed. He scrambled up quickly.

"On your stomach, spread-eagled," she said.

He stretched out on the bed face down and waited. She moved around the bed, gently putting the heavy leather cuffs on his wrists and ankles, and attaching them to the bedposts, hardly touching him. The only sounds in the room were his breathing and the gentle clink of the buckles and clips as she attached them.

She stepped back from him. He turned awkwardly to look around at her and she shook her head at him without a word. He obediently closed his eyes and lowered his face to the bed, and he waited. She watched him for a few moments, so beautiful. He started an almost imperceptible trembling, small beads of perspiration formed on his back and neck. She knew the silence was scaring him a little and that his mind was racing, trying to anticipate what was coming.

She let him wait, eyeing her toys, trying to decide what she was in the mood for. She moved around the room silently, restless, discarding her clothes as she paced.

She took off her g-string last, bunched it up into a ball and approached the bed, still scanning the room for inspiration. She almost absentmindedly brought her panties to his lips, his mouth opening automatically so that she could shove them in, pushing them with her fingers until she knew they were sitting in the back of his mouth. She traced his lips with her fingers, feeling their softness while she dismissed each of her floggers and paddles as not fitting her mood.

Finally she got onto the bed and lay down full-length on top of him, spreading herself across his back. He sighed as the weight of her anchored him. She wriggled against him, making contact with his skin from her feet to her pussy, to her breasts, to her arms, to her cheek against the back of his head. She lay there, still, feeling his heartbeat against her chest, breathing into his ear, absorbing his heat.

She licked his shoulder, nuzzling into his neck, kissing the soft skin there. He shifted to give her better access to the sensitive spot. She increased the pressure of her lips, the intensity of her kisses. He shuddered as she sucked and nipped at his neck and she felt him start to writhe under her. She felt the pull in her stomach as she started to draw his skin into her mouth and clamp down on it harder, her hunger rising.

She sat up, straddled his arse, pushing her wet pussy against him. She bared her teeth, a feral smile. And then she began to bite him.

What started as nips and nibbles at his neck grew quickly savage, turning into vicious animal bites at his exposed flesh. She pulled large chunks of skin on his shoulder, his back, into her mouth and closed her teeth on it as if she would tear it from his bones. She felt him trying to pull away from her, but there was nowhere to go, and his wriggling and his soft grunts spurred her on.

Her mouth moved all over his back, every part of him, leaving large red marks that would surely bruise. She travelled down to his arse, biting his cheeks. She felt like she was grinding his skin between her jaws.

She felt his hips rocking against the bed as her mouth moved over his arse. She heard herself making a low growling sound as her mouth found unmarked flesh. She wanted to swallow chunks of his flesh, to own it, to eat it. He had started to whimper softly as she moved across his body, and the whimpering was soon accentuated by grunts of pain as she relentlessly continued. She wanted to mark him all over, and she continued for a long time until barely a spot on his back or arse was untouched.

She knelt back on the bed beside him when she was sated and studied her handiwork: his back and arse covered in a series of red, angry looking teeth marks. She touched them, feeling the indentations, stroking the redness, gently measuring the heat of the angry skin. He moaned softly as her fingertips travelled tenderly over the damaged skin.

Her hand skipped down to his bitten arse, and her fingers trailed down to his balls. She stroked him gently, he lifted his hips slightly towards her, tried to widen his legs to give her better access.

"Lift up for me, boy," she said, and he obediently lifted his arse up to her as much as his bonds would allow.

She slid her hand under his body to touch his cock; it was rock hard, pulsing under her touch. She ran her fingers along the hardness to the tip and felt him move his hips to try and increase the contact with her hand.

She smiled.

"Let's turn you over," she said. "I'm not done yet."

Meeting

They had been in touch online and by phone for quite a while already. He was funny and smart. He fitted. She liked his openness despite it not being his nature, his hints of shyness, his obvious desire to submit to her, his sense of humour. Even his inexperience had appeal.

In the last week before meeting, he seemed to be having doubts. She sensed his skittishness, like a racehorse balking at the gate. She was travelling specifically to meet him and made compromises to reassure him, and to ensure that the meeting happened. She felt disadvantaged, vulnerable, but she did it anyway, hoping she would not regret it.

She arrived before the meeting and checked into the hotel. When she got to the room, she prepared, just in case. She anchored the perfect lengths of rope to the corners of the bed, and within convenient reach placed heavy leather wrist cuffs, ankle cuffs, clips, a blindfold and a ruler. She placed soap and moisturiser in the bathroom and put some towels on the tiled floor where she planned to have him kneel if all went well. The preparations excited her. Thinking about how she was going to use him with each piece made her head spin.

She slipped into her g-string and bra, jeans, black belt, black fitted t-shirt and drew on her knee high stiletto 'fuck me' boots enjoying the extra inches it added to her considerable height, putting her at about 6'2. She wasn't nervous to be meeting him, but she was anxious about her own reaction, fearing she would want it too much, want him too much, or alternatively fearing she would feel nothing at all.

She went to the bar, ordered a drink. She was a little early. He walked in shortly afterwards, finding her quickly. She smiled and stood, greeting him with an outstretched hand, leaning in for a kiss on the cheek.

He sat across from her, and said he had had to run to make it on time. She smiled and looked at her watch. He was 2 minutes early.

She examined his face as he caught his breath, leaning back, his legs outstretched. He looked better than his photo, and he was clean shaven for her as was her preference. At 6' and lean, he was just her type. His hair was dark brown, his eyes also dark, edged with a crinkling that hinted at a sense of mischief.

They talked about nothing much, chit chat, feeling each other out. He had a lovely mouth, full lips, great teeth. She watched it as they talked, assessing how much she wanted it. The only hints at why they were there were vague references to things they had discussed online, and she made him show her how he checked what colour boxers he had on, a ritual question she had imposed remotely. She watched as he pulled his shirt up, sucked in his abs, and pulled the waist of his jeans away from his body to look down.

"Show me," she said.

He leaned over, pulling his charcoal boxers up a little so that she could see. She smiled and nodded, feeling a pull in her stomach.

After about an hour of talking, and quite a bit of laughter, she asked him, "What do you think?"

He nodded, smiled. "I think it's going well, good rapport... what do you think?"

She nodded back, agreeing.

They were getting on well and she felt the hunger, soft and low, humming.

The conversation slowed as she started to consider if she wanted to play with him. By this time, the bar had started to fill, and he had moved closer to her. He was within her reach now.

She leaned forward and beckoned him to come to her. He brought his face closer to hers and her hand snaked around his neck, caressing him, her fingers finding purchase in his hair, her fist closing. She saw him wince as she pulled his hair into her grip and tightened her hold. She moved his head from left to right, he looked down and closed his eyes, a soft "Ow" leaving his mouth, the sound resonating in her. She smiled and pulled his face to hers, stroking his cheek with her cheek, breathing into his ear.

She released him and put her hand on his leg, her fingers sliding into the creases of his jeans behind his knee. He looked down at her hand on him.

"You have nice hands," he commented, oddly.

She smiled, he was nervous.

She leaned forward in her seat, looking intently at him, silent, her mind working overtime, weighing up the pros and cons of playing with him, staring at his mouth, imagining taking it with her mouth, considering him without speaking. The heavy silence and the staring made him increasingly uncomfortable, and he squirmed under her gaze, not knowing where to look as the moments stretched.

She seemed unconcerned about his obvious discomfort, in fact she enjoyed it, it fed her hunger. She imagined inviting him upstairs, played the scene out in her head and tried to assess how it made her feel, still looking intently at his face. Her heartbeat quickened as she made a decision.

Finally, she beckoned him and he brought his face to hers. She held him there with a hand behind his neck. She rubbed her cheek against his.

She hesitated, then put her mouth to his ear and whispered, "Do you want to come upstairs and take some clothes off for me?"

She felt him tense, but his response was immediate.

"Yes Ma'am," he said, quietly, deliberately, clearly into her ear.

She felt her pussy twitch... it was the first time he had called her 'Ma'am' to her face.

"Are you sure?" she whispered.

"Yes Ma'am," he repeated and her heart melted just a little.

She nodded, stood up and gestured for him to follow.

She stalked ahead, and held her hand out behind her without looking back. She felt him slip his hand into hers, warm and compliant, and her stomach lurched with lust as she closed her fingers around his, leading him towards the foyer. She pictured him obediently following as she headed for the lifts.

Strip, boy

As soon as the door closes behind us, I am on you.

I shove you back against the wall, grab a fistful of your hair, jerk your head back, then sideways. Your eyes widen, you try not to resist. Your head smashes against the wood as I push myself up against you, my mouth on yours. I open my mouth, forcing your lips apart, I suck your breath, your arms automatically go around my waist as you pull me harder against you and seek out my tongue with yours.

You strain forward against my grip in your hair to get more of my mouth. I pull harder on your hair, reaching for you at the same time as I keep you from getting more of me. I push my hips forward to get contact with your cock, wanting to feel it harden against me, I grind my pelvis against you, close, closer, not close enough.

I pull away suddenly, your head still held back by my fingers twisted in your hair. Your whole body strains to get at me, but you know better than to try. We are both breathing hard, I release my grip on you.

"Hands behind your head," I say.

You immediately comply, locking your fingers behind your head, your eyes on me.

I step back, looking you up and down, seeing the outline of your cock hard against the front of your jeans. You wait, watching me, awkward, slightly self-conscious under the scrutiny. I see you struggling not to make a smart arse remark into the silence, you are uncomfortable, want to break the tension. I savour your unease, taking my time.

"Strip, boy."

You keep your eyes on me as you quickly shed your clothes, throw them aside and stand back in position.

Raw

I am sandpapered and roughened, I can't get close enough to consume you. My skin is raw from trying to swallow you.

I make you bring your mouth to me like an offering. I spread myself over you like I can force myself into you if I push hard enough. I suck your lips into my mouth and close my teeth on them. I taste your blood and push my tongue against that openness. I turn your head upside down so I can suck the sweetness off your tongue. I make you reach for me and lick gently at your open mouth. I twist your head into unnatural positions so that I can get inside you. I shove you back and pull you hard against me to devour you. I hold my fingers to your throat to push you away and hear you choke yourself to get to me. I try to rip your tongue out of your mouth and feel you offer it up. I shove my mouth and nose against you to stop you breathing never breaking the kiss. I clash my teeth into your softness and wait for that wincing moan.

I pull away, eventually, and reluctantly, and when I do, you reach for me, eyes closed, mouth half open, tongue against your sore and bloody swollen lips, your breath ragged and desperate, you reach for me.

Good morning

I feel the bed shift as you lean over to sneak a look at my face, quietly checking to see if I am stirring yet. I've been awake for a while, half dozing in that soft space between sleep and consciousness, but I keep my eyes closed. It amuses me to make you wait, I can feel your impatience crackling between us, the silent entreaty, "Come ON!"

When I finally open my eyes sleepily and gaze over at you. Your face lights up with pleasure, we share a silent moment of sweet connection. You know that once I am awake you are allowed to kiss my exposed skin, bare above the sheet. You start with a tender kiss on my shoulder, all soft lips and warm breath.

The kissing is both a greeting and a gentle feeling out of my mood. Sometimes I grunt and barely acknowledge you, turning rudely away. Sometimes I purr and arch into your kisses exposing the side of my neck, that tender skin under my ear to you. Sometimes I pull the sheet down and roll over so you can reach my back, my arse. Sometimes I grab at you when I feel your mouth on me and shove you into some position that pleases me and wrap my legs around you and sink my teeth into whatever pieces of your flesh are within reach.

On this particular Saturday morning, I stretch luxuriously under your attention, feeling my muscles wake up. I pull your face down close to me, my mouth at your ear.

"Good morning," I whisper.

I hear the smile in your reply. "Good morning, Ma'am."

"I want to come in your mouth," I say softly.

You make a small sound of pleasure. "Yes, Ma'am!"

You have to seduce me, even though I've clearly told you what I want. You have to kiss and lick and suck and stroke and tease me into it. You have learnt how my body works, you are good at pleasuring it, your mouth travelling slowly downwards, paying attention to the sensitive areas.

Licking and nibbling at my nipples, feeling them harden against your tongue. That spot just below my ribs that makes me gasp when you make as if to bite me. You linger at my inner thighs, nuzzling the sensitive skin there, moving slowly to brush against my pussy as if by accident, ignoring how my hips lift up off the bed towards your mouth. A frustrated hiss escapes my lips, but you don't relent. Soft kisses and light touches light up my body until all of my focus is on getting more. And finally... there of course, you reach out with your tongue to play against my clit.

You barely touch me with your tongue at first, an excruciating tease that I love. You wait to give my clit concentrated attention until I am arching up, lifting my hips off the bed towards you, making soft desperate sounds. You wait until you become worried that you will misjudge and I will tip over from the pleasure of anticipation into impatience. Timing it just right so that you don't misinterpret the signals is a skill, and you sometimes still get it wrong and get a slap instead of an 'ohgodyes' sigh.

This time though, you are perfect, exactly right. Your tongue laps at my clit and I growl under the attention, and settle back down on the bed, reaching a hand down to grab a fistful of your hair. A reassurance, an encouragement. You moan against me when I use the grip to hold you still and rub my pussy up against your face.

I want to touch you a little while your mouth is busy. All supine and still half asleep, my hips pushing my pussy up against your tongue, I want your cock.

"Bring my cock here where I can reach it," I say.

You know better than to stop kissing or licking or stroking while you comply. You manoeuvre yourself, shifting awkwardly from your comfortable position lying between my legs, getting up on all fours and bringing your arse and cock within reach of my hand, your mouth anchored between my legs, your tongue never losing the rhythm against my clit.

I lazily reach out to play with your cock without any particular intent. I just like touching you. A pinch, a gentle smack, a squeeze if your mouth distracts me. I like how you react to it, feeling the pressure against my clit change when you go 'oh', your tongue stilling for a moment if I hurt you.

I just barely touch your cock, my fingertips rubbing against that sensitive spot under the head, a little pressure, a little stroke, just to watch your body react. Desperate for more contact, you try to push against me somehow, your hips thrusting to try and force your cock harder against my fingers. The hot desperation in it makes me shove my pussy tighter up against your mouth.

You concentrate on making me come, trying not to be distracted by my hand on your cock. You feel my body tense as I get close, the muscles in my thighs tightening, my moans drop an octave signalling that I'm on the edge. I convulsively close my fingers around your cock as I fuck up into your mouth. My tightening grip on your cock makes you moan against me.

I grab your hair again, holding you right there, and go with the rising waves of my orgasm as I come, my thighs squeezing tightly, holding your face tight up against me as the waves take hold, forcing your mouth hard up against me, carrying you with me as my entire body lifts up off the bed and twists sideways.

I curl up for a moment, catching my breath, your head still trapped between my thighs until I relax and allow you freedom.

Fully awake now, I pull you up to me by your hair so I can have your mouth. Your cock is still hard and I trap it between my thighs, against my pussy, which is now wet and sensitive and slick. That pressure is perfect in the aftermath of my orgasm, and I can't get enough of your mouth, pulling your body against me, my nails digging into your skin. I keep adjusting my position against you while you thrust deliberately and slowly into the slickness at the junction of my thighs and my pussy. Your strong hands hold my full body length against you, conjoined at the cock and the mouth.

I grind against you and you finally beg me to stop because you know you are not allowed to come and oh god, you are so close. I love that: Knowing how much you want to come, yet begging me not to. If your beautiful desperation is enough to make me want to come again, then that's your job. Though sometimes I will just do it myself, my fingers on my clit and against your cock so you can feel it second hand, my mouth on yours so you can taste my moans when I come.

When I've had my fill, I untangle myself from you and head to the shower. I hear you scramble to get up and follow me. I smile, anticipating your strong soapy hands as you wash me.

Nightly spanking

I tell him to get the paddle. He returns to where I am sitting on the edge of the bed, kneels before me and offers it up to me. I smile at him, he gives me a cheeky look back.

"Spanking, baby..." I announce, unnecessarily.

"But... but... I've been a good boy!" he mock-protests, his eyes wide.

I laugh. He is funny.

I cup his face to me and kiss him gently. He leans into it, and I feel his body relax at the familiar intimacy.

I take my t-shirt off and slip my pants down my legs: I want to feel every inch of his skin against me. He waits before me, watching quietly. I touch him under his t-shirt, sliding the fabric up and he lifts his arms so that I can slip it over his head, his gesture is childlike and sweet.

I pat my lap and he lays his body across my thighs, heavy and warm. I reach to pull his pants down so that they are around his knees, exposing his arse to me. I pull him tight against me, my stomach against his side, his cock (mine) and thighs against my leg. I enjoy his solid warmth and stroke the skin of his back, down to his rounded cheeks over and over, touching his warm smooth skin.

I start with my fingers, stroking and tapping gently against his arse for a short while before delivering a hard slap to his right cheek. I feel his body jump a little at the first one, a shock even though he knows it's coming. Then I start to spank him in earnest, concentrating on the sound and feel of him under my hand. I smack him in rhythmic spurts... slap-pat-slap-pat-SLAP-SLAPSLAPSLAPSLAP-pat-pat. Then again, and again. Each time a little different. His skin warms under my hand, he starts to make soft "ow" noises as his skin becomes sensitive, even though I know there is no real pain in it. His body sways against me with each strike.

I use different rhythms to give my hand a rest. It hurts me if I hit too hard for too long: I am delicate like that, but I enjoy very much the skin-on-skin contact and am reluctant to use the paddle. He curls tightly against me, and I realise he is trying to get his mouth on my leg. I widen my knees and feel him nuzzle and kiss my thigh as I continue to spank his arse. I feel his lips form the "ow" sound against my skin. I feel the little expulsion of air when I hit him particularly hard. His skin reddens prettily, his body rocking against me.

When my hand gets a little sore, I smack him gently along the crack of his arse down to his balls. He widens his stance to give me better access and makes sounds of pain at the gentle slapping to those sensitive spots. His body moves against me, his cock hard against my thigh. I don't use the paddle. I spank him until my hand is red and sore and his arse feels hot under my fingers.

I finish by pulling him close against me, stroking him down, petting his hair, leaning over him, covering him with my body to get as much contact as I can against him. He relaxes against me, his breathing heavy.

When I tell him to kneel up, he does so slowly, his face is open, dazed, soft. He is made heartbreakingly small by this: spanking makes him feel vulnerable and exposed. I widen my knees and pull him close close close. He wraps his arms around me, both of us trying to get as much contact as possible. We stroke and kiss for a long time, reluctant to break the spell. Finally, though, we tumble into bed.

Wash me

He was kneeling on the edge of the bed. She put a blindfold on him, smoothing the silk over his eyes. Unable to resist his mouth, she kissed him again, nudging at his lips, soft kisses, opening his mouth with hers, gently licking at his tongue, holding him at the back of his neck to bring him to her. His mouth searched for her as she pulled away.

"Undress me," she said.

He felt blindly for her fitted t-shirt, and pulled it up over her head. His fingers gently touched her skin, tracing her bra to the clasp at the back. He struggled to undo it. She remained silent, still, a smile on her face as she felt him start to get frustrated with it.

It finally came undone and he sighed with relief and pulled it off, her breasts free, nipples hardening in the cool air.

He moved on to her jeans; her belt and zipper already loosened, though he couldn't remember how that had happened. He pulled them down over her hips, but couldn't reach further from his position on the bed. She sat on the bed beside him, then leaned back to hold her legs up in front of him, touching his chest with them. He felt the weight of them as she relaxed against him, reached for the top of her jeans and pulled, intending to slide them off. She smirked as it took a moment for him to realise that they were tucked into her boots.

She pushed him backwards gently with pressure on his chest and he sat back on his heels. She lowered her legs into his lap.

He touched her knee-high boot, running his fingers from the pointed toe, feeling for the zipper on the inside leg. He pulled the zipper down, grabbed the bottom of the boot and awkwardly tried to pull it off.

"By the heel," she whispered.

He nodded, pulling at the stiletto heel, the boot slipping off. He repeated the process with the other boot. He stroked her warm feet softly for a second.

His hands then gently felt their way back up her legs, tugging awkwardly on her jeans to slide them down her legs and off. His fingertips travelled lightly back up her legs, feather touches, finding the soft fabric of her panties at her crotch, following the seam to her hips. He slid his fingers into the sides of her g-string and she lifted her arse off the bed to allow him to pull them down also.

She got up off the bed and stood naked before his blindfolded eyes. She pulled him to her, pressed her body up against him, holding his hands behind his back, feeling the warmth of skin on skin, the wetness on his boxers against her hip. He pushed forward against her to get more contact, she took his mouth again, tenderly tasting him. She couldn't get enough of it. He was delicious.

She pulled him off the bed so that he was standing before her.

"Take off your boxers."

He complied quickly, and her eyes travelled his naked body; lean, hard, expectant, his shallow breaths making his body vibrate. His nervous expression made her hunger, made her want his mouth again, but she refrained. Instead, she took both of his hands in hers and led him carefully and slowly into the bathroom. She put him into position in front of the open shower door and pushed him down to the floor to kneel.

"Wash me," she said, and put a pump pack of liquid soap into his hand as she stepped into the shower, turning it on.

He made his hands soapy, and leaned into the shower to wash her. She watched him concentrating, his cock hard as he reached blindly for her. He found her thigh, but moved down quickly to start at her feet, she lifted them for him and he washed first one, then the other with care. His hands slid, soapy, up her legs—gently, yet insistently moving up one leg, then down the other, and again, slipping over her wet body, glancing over her pussy.

His touch left her as he lathered up with more soap, his hands ran over her stomach, his fingers spread, reaching up to her breasts. His touch made her nipples harden, and he caught them briefly between his fingers before moving up to her shoulders, then down first one arm then the other. His hands were gliding again and again up and down her body until she turned to let him reach her back.

He pressed his fingers harder against her shoulders, the small of her back and gentle again over her arse, slipping gently between her cheeks, and back down her legs.

When he was done, he pulled back, kneeling up at the entrance to the shower.

"Okay Ma'am?" he asked.

She ignored him and rinsed, turning the shower off when she finished.

"Sit back on your heels."

He did as he was told, his unseeing eyes tilted up towards her. She stepped out of the shower and stood over him, dripping water onto his skin. She looked down at his blindfolded face, gripped his hair in her fist and took a half step forward, pushing his head backwards, she stepped over him, suddenly shoving her pussy against his mouth.

He immediately opened his mouth and started licking at her. Watching him made her crazy, his head bent back, half of his face obscured by her pussy, the other half covered by the blindfold. He looked unrecognisable, anonymous, his mouth and tongue desperately working to please her. She rocked against him, rubbing against his mouth as he lapped at her, her breath quickening.

She leaned back from him. The pressure wasn't quite what she wanted.

"Stick out your tongue," she said softly.

He complied quickly, and she held his head still by his hair and slid her pussy up and down on his tongue. She moved his head backwards and forwards in rhythm with her movements, his tongue sliding against her over and again. She knew he was dying to lick at her, but he obediently kept his tongue out and still as she rubbed herself against it. She tried to keep silent as she increased the rhythm of her movements, feeling the familiar rise of growing need.

With a soft moan, she pulled away from him. His face was wet, from the water or from her pussy, it was impossible to tell.

He kept his mouth open, his tongue out, waiting for her to come back to him, straining towards her.

She passed him a towel and felt his disappointment as he dried her carefully.

"Moisturiser," she said, and she caught his smile as he eagerly held out his hand for the lotion.

She handed it to him, and he started, again, at her feet.

Kissing him

I sit on the arm of the couch and look down at him. I stroke his face. I place my hand on his cheek and cup his face up to me as I kiss him gently. He kisses me back tentatively, and I nudge his mouth open, tasting him. It rises quickly in me, passion, heat.

I kiss him a little harder, exploring his mouth, my fingers slip to his throat, applying some pressure, pushing his head back, tilting it until it is along the back of the couch, and I kiss him, tasting him, feeling the skin of his exposed throat under my fingers. I kiss him harder, biting his lips, feeling him wince, feeling like I can't breathe. And I kiss him harder and he returns my aggression, his mouth hungry, wanting, I slip my finger between his lips without breaking the kiss, feeling his tongue, his teeth. I kiss him harder, I can't get enough.

He is stroking me, running his hand cautiously along my arm as I lean further over him, his hand along the side of my body, I grip his hair and hold his head back, he strokes my side, across my ribs, my breast, I push him back along the couch, eating up his mouth, shoving his head back, I feel like growling and I can't get enough of his mouth. I am almost lying over him, pushing at him, his head arched back against the back of the couch, kissing, pushing, wanting.

I pull back finally, slowing, just touching his lips with mine, lapping at his soft bottom lip, pulling it gently into my mouth, my breathing ragged, pulling a few inches away, thinking I am finished with him.

He whispers, "You are such a great kisser."

"So are you," I answer. And it's true.

"This was so worth it," I tell him, but I am not finished with him yet.

He looks up at me and he knows I am not done with him, and I feel him reach for me, and I let him guide my mouth gently back down to his, like guiding a missile to its target, like guiding me home, and once I am locked, I am lost again, and I nudge against his mouth, finding his tongue, aggressively taking his mouth, and feeling like I can't get enough.

I feel a soft pressure as he tries to urge me off the arm of the couch into his lap, against his body. I resist, keeping my mouth on his, pushing. I grip his hair tightly in my fingers and he lets out a little moan and I twist his head back further and pull away to look at his face, his eyes are closed, supplication, surrender, submission. I touch my fingertips to his lips and he opens his mouth, I enter with my finger, fingers, he keeps his eyes closed and he wraps his lips around my fingers, he sucks them and I slide them in and out of his mouth, feeling his tongue lapping at them, watching, wanting, perfect and it makes my hunger rise, my stomach lurching with lust. And I kiss him hard and it's delicious, and I feel voracious and he is pushing up against me with his mouth, wanting more, and I feel like I want to get inside him through his mouth.

I start to slow a little and pull away, I gently touch his lips with my tongue, he reaches up for me and I pull back further and he arches up to me and he can't get to my mouth and I make him wait for me before I can't bear not to have my mouth on his anymore, and I move down to kiss him, hard, again, and I make a sound, like a moan deep in my throat and I feel him react to it even though I never heard it escape my lips. I feel like I am kissing him forever.

I finally slow my attack on him, pause and pull away from him.

I whisper, "You're lovely."

He doesn't hear me. I repeat it.

He smiles up at me.

He waits

He stands in position, his hands clasped behind his head, his feet shoulder width apart. He stretches his body, pulls his navel towards his spine, holds his muscles taut; his abs, his biceps, his thighs all slightly flexed: He knows she likes that.

And he waits.

He concentrates on keeping still, quelling his urge to shift, to fidget. He knows better. He listens for any sound, any hint that she is approaching. Time passes slowly.

And he waits.

His mind wanders, he is thinking about her, forming her image in his mind, hearing her voice, feeling her touch, his cock starts to harden. He wills it down, feeling his face warm, flush with embarrassment. His mind registers the blush: he knows she likes that, and the knowing makes his cock jerk and harden further. His stomach starts to flutter, butterflies, part fear, part anticipation. He closes his mouth to prevent a low moan from escaping his lips.

And he waits.

Putting him to bed

I put you to bed at 5am, some four hours ago, and I am thinking about you now. I'm trying to work, instead, I am thinking about you, naked and tied, thinking about you saying "Thank you Ma'am" to me, thinking about you, and it's incredibly hot.

I have the entire reel in my head and I play it with different themes (hard, hissy, snarly 'get on that bed now, boy' with slapping and spitting; or it being all about sex, scratchy, grabby, rubbing, wet; or it being sweet, soft, gentle, coaxing, kissing), all a little different, all hugely sexy in their own way and I am not sure which I like best. Though you were doe-eyed and sleepy, and your "Is that okay?" made me melt, so it was more sweet than anything, this putting you to bed.

"Take off your boxers, baby, and lie down there for me."

Stroking you, touching that bruise you have, the purple one, leaning down to kiss it, unable to resist sinking my teeth in to hear you gasp.

I whisper, "Sorry baby," and laugh softly.

Sitting on the centre of the bed, the sole reason for which is to lie over your chest and stretch along you as

I wrap your yellow tie around your wrist, you watch me, leaning on you as I knot it, checking that it's tight, jerking your wrist against it, then lifting your arm to check how much room you have to move. Leaning then over your lower body, feeling you hard against me as I'm lying across you to reach your ankle, wrapping your blue silk tie around it, and securing it to the bed, pulling it to make sure it's not going to come undone.

Coming back up to look at your face, you give me a half smile, you look sweet, grateful, vulnerable, expectant. Lying full length on top of you, feeling the warmth of your skin through my clothes, holding both of your hands above your head, fingers entwined, my legs on top of your legs, and yes, I can feel your cock and I shift against it, reaching up for your mouth. Just touching my lips to yours, soft, barely there, a tiny taste of you with my tongue, nudging against your mouth, which makes you crane your neck towards me to try and deepen the kiss, and I press up against your mouth and kiss you hard, my tongue finding yours and forcing your mouth open a little more so I can get further inside you.

And I kiss you for a long time, hearing soft inarticulate sounds of pleasure, yours or mine, I can't tell, and I can feel you shifting under me, your hips tensing, wanting to push up against me, but you know that's likely to stop the kissing, so you hold back. And it's your bedtime and you are tired, can barely keep your eyes open, though I know you wouldn't argue if I was to stay there, kissing you. And I finally whisper goodnight and I stroke your face and check the bindings before I leave, locking the door behind me.

I wonder if you drifted off, but given you don't sleep well at the best of times, I doubt it. I imagine you are hard, uncomfortable, exhausted, unable to sleep and you are starting to think this is going to be difficult, and I know you want to do this for me, and you are squirming, shuffling, feeling the ties, and kind of liking that, but wondering if you are going to get any sleep at all, maybe wondering why you said yes to this, asked for it even.

And that, all that, is incredibly hot for me, imagining you there, tethered to your bed, naked, doing this for me. Delicious.

Card Game

I pass you some cards, face down on the table and wait for you to select one and turn it up, watching your expression as you do. And it makes me smile because of course what is on the cards is random, scary, fun, silly, painful, horrible, delicious.

For once, I let you keep your clothes on because it makes you feel safe and protected, and the cards will take care of that soon enough, if you choose one that does, take care of that. And some of those cards will elicit a huge smile and a touch of relief and a softening of those pretty eyes, and that would be lovely. And some of them will make you hard, make you lick your lips, make you moan softly, and god, I would love that. And some of them will make you glance quickly up, and then back down, wanting to put it back on the table, but that's not an option.

And if you pick one of those cards, the third type, maybe you would hold it in your hands, close to you, resisting turning it to show me what you had chosen, and I would wait, and in the waiting I would start to lean forward, watching your face and you would look at me with a slight shake of your head and a furrow in your brow, and that would make me start to hunger. I would wait and hold your gaze and the longer you took, the more I would want to see it, that card.

And if you hesitated long enough, and looked unsure enough, and your breathing was getting ragged because you were thinking about what was on the card, I might lean right across the table, and shove you backwards with my mouth on yours, feeling your chair start to tip. Pushing anyway, with my mouth on yours, feeling teeth clash, which would make us both wince, not caring, just wanting it, your mouth.

And still you would be holding the card, maybe crushing it a little between us, kissing me back. I would growl deep in my throat, your lips moving under mine, tasting your tongue, and god the kissing, so fucking good. And you would maybe release thoughts of the card, though it would still be there, getting crushed in your fingers.

Until I pulled away, and I looked at your hand still holding the card, and I would look back into your face.

"Show me," I would say.

THE COUCH

He slid off the couch and sat at her feet. He lowered his cheek to her knee and rested there. She idly stroked his face, running her fingers through his hair, he rubbed his cheek almost imperceptibly against her leg as she stroked him. She could almost imagine him purring, but he was silent, his eyes closed as she petted him. Her hand left him to turn a page of her book, and she felt him sink down to the floor. He lay there, shifting, squirming, trying to find a position that would make him feel warm and safe; gently, silently trying to find a way to get closer to her.

He squeezed himself behind her legs and wrapped his body around her, he pulled her legs into him, curled there on the floor. She shifted her feet, pulling him back against the couch, applying a little pressure to his stomach so he could feel her more strongly, bringing him closer. He was foetal around her feet and he held on to her legs as if she was going to float away. His fingers touched her feet and calves gently, not quite stroking, almost as if he was reassuring himself that she was still there.

She turned another page in the silence.

First time

The very first time I went out to any kind of public BDSM-related event, it was a 'BDSM night' at a Goth club. It was the first time I had identified as a 'Domme' in public: I had never been to a BDSM club before, had no idea what to expect, had never played with a submissive, didn't have a clue what I was doing.

I wore a black catsuit, a wide belt that was essentially a waist cincher, killer stiletto boots, my brightest red lipstick, and I had my multi-strand flogger in my bag.

The club was open to the public, but the BDSM activity was in a separate room from the main area. When we got there, we scoped it out, grabbed drinks and found a bench to sit on so that we could watch what was going on.

I had explored online prior to this, which is a common enough experience. I was shocked to find that real life mirrored the online world in a lot of ways. Submissive men came up to me, dropped to their knees before a word had left their mouths, and they asked me to do 'things' to and with them. Various things, random things. Mostly I said "No", but in amongst the strangeness of it was a little thrill.

While most of the early part of the night disappeared from memory a long time ago, I recall two things in particular.

The first was an older gentleman coming up and asking if I would 'take him out the back' and choke him so that he couldn't breathe. I was so shocked by the idea that he would ask a total stranger whose skills he had no idea of to do this that I'm sure I spluttered my response, but he got a resounding "Oh hell no!"

The second was a man who knelt before my friend and asked her to slap his face. She said no, then gestured to me, "She'll do it." She smirked at me as she said it. He dutifully turned to me and asked me to please slap his face. I looked at him for a few moments, considering it. I was nervous about it, but it was something I'd always wanted to try. I said yes, and slapped him tentatively across the cheek. I got an immediate, and shocking rush from it. It was thrilling.

"Harder... harder!" he ordered, not even really pretending that it was anything other than me fulfilling his fantasy.

I obliged, slapping him again and harder, while internally going "Oh wow!". I don't think I hit him as hard as he wanted, but for me, the sensation of it was surprising, incredible.

I became bolder with trying different things as I felt more comfortable during the night, though the detail of those activities has become lost with time.

Quite late in the evening, two arrogant, cocky,

smirking men sauntered over with their girlfriends. They were not Goths, were not dressed in fetish attire: They wore jeans, plain shirts, perhaps had wandered in off the street.

"We want you to whip us," one of them said to me.

"I beg your pardon?" It was the rudest request I had received all night.

"We want you to whip us... You're the house Domme aren't you?"

House Domme? Who knew there was such a thing? I cannot at all recall what I had been doing that made them think I was one, but I was obviously making the most of my first night out.

"No, I'm not. If I do it, I do it because I want to."

"Well, we want you to whip us."

I scowled. "Like I have the slightest interest in what you want..."

The conversation, such as it was, progressed from there to me acting like das über bitch in the face of their demands.

In the end, I made them both get down on their knees and beg me to whip them. They were still all cocky and smirking, treating it like a joke, but they did it. I made them keep begging until they started to look quite uncomfortable, and I was satisfied.

I don't remember flogging the first boy. He was almost irrelevant, though I recall sitting with him afterwards. He was shaky, I made someone get him some water.

The second boy, now he was something else.

There were cuffs suspended from hooks in the ceiling: I made him take his shirt off and cuffed him up, stretched. He was looking at his girlfriend, smiling, mugging, showing off for her.

I pressed up against him and whispered that this was going to hurt. He smirked at me as I started to hit him on his upper back with the flogger. Soft at first. Finding my rhythm. Easing him in.

I did a lot of stroking when I paused. I ran my fingertips across his back, his chest, along the waistband of his jeans, pressed my body full length up to him, pushing against him, bringing my mouth right up close to his, intently watching his face.

I hit him harder and harder, and he started to flinch with every stroke. He started to pay attention. He stopped smirking. He stopped looking at his girlfriend. His eyes followed me as I moved around him. I forgot about anyone else being there. My world was reduced to just me and him.

I continued to hit him, starting to put some force behind it, watching his skin change colour under it. I became more and more comfortable with the flogger, trying different angles, different levels of force.

His girlfriend came up to me when I paused.

"Can I touch him?" she asked.

I didn't even look at her. "No." I dismissed her, waved her away, she was a distraction.

For now, for this, he was mine.

Between the hitting, there was a lot of stroking of his bare skin, pressing the length of my body against his, whispering.

"Does it hurt?" I asked him softly, breathing into his ear.

He looked at me, nodding, whispering, "Yes."

I brought my face close to his, my mouth an inch away from his lips, we shared breaths. And with the pain and the stroking and the whispering, he was hard. He started to beg me to kiss him, his body reaching for me against his restraints.

"Kiss me, please kiss me... please..."

I continued to hit him, his whole body rocking against the force of the blows. I watched his face. He was totally flying, glazed eyes locked on me with longing, every fibre of him straining to get to me, increasingly desperate.

"Please, please kiss me please kiss me..."

I ignored his entreaty, ran my fingers around the waistband of his jeans. I looked into his face as he melted into the touch. I popped open the top button and he looked quizzically at me. Slowly I took down the zip, probing fingers glancing against the outline of his cock. He blushed, he stammered that his pants would fall down. Lightly protesting at first, then genuinely worried when he saw that I wasn't reacting.

"Please don't let my jeans fall down... please."

He widened his stance to hold his jeans more firmly in place, an edge of panic in his voice that amused me. I smirked at him. He was hard. He was scared of being humiliated. And still his eyes followed me as I moved around him, and still he reached for me with his body, with his mouth, straining against the cuffs. And he didn't really know what to beg for, but the kissing won out again.

"Please kiss me... please please kiss me..."

As I beat him and circled him, I watched his face. It was so incredibly beautiful: begging, grunting with pain, cheeks flushed, inarticulate noises coming out of his mouth. And through it all, his cock straining against his open fly.

I continued to hit him and touch him and whisper to him until I had had enough.

When I stopped, and let him down, he was shaking. He was totally high on endorphins and his face was one of shock, his eyes glassy. He looked at me with awe and wonder. I sat with him in the aftermath, petting him down, murmuring nothing to him, trying to make sense of what had just happened between us.

When I left the club shortly after that, both boys came out and literally followed my girlfriend and me down the street chanting my name as if we were in some strange art-house movie where things like that actually happen (truly bizarre).

As for me, I had never never NEVER felt anything like it. It was like a revelation.

It wasn't about hurting him, it was about moving him through that transition: the way he went from an arrogant, cocky, smirking vanilla jerk to a begging, wanting, beautifully vulnerable 'thing'. The power of creating that, the hotness and beauty in it was incredible, indescribable. Add to that the concentration of energy, how totally lost in it I was, how there was no-one else there except me and him, how there was nothing else except that moment right there, and then the next one.

It totally blew my mind.

And I thought, "I have got to get me some more of that."

Show me how to hurt you

"I've never done this before, you have to show me."

"Yes Ma'am, I'll show you, here...like this, you can do it like this..."

"Like this, boy?"

"No, you can do it tighter... there... and then..."

"Tight enough now? And what if I do it up this way? How's that?"

"That's good... nice... but you can be much rougher with me. You are holding back."

"Yes, yes, I am... until I see the impact... Okay... this? How's this now?"

"Yes, that's good, pretty good, and then you can use this to add pressure there..."

"Here... like this...? I can tell that you like that..."

"Well, just you fucking with me, I like that regardless Ma'am... Oh! But that... Oh...! Yes...!"

"That hit something didn't it, boy?"

"Oh yes... that's... nice... maybe you could also do this Ma'am, at the same time there..."

"There? Hard like that?"

"Oh...! Jeessus! Ummm... yes!!! Ohhh...!!"

"And this...?"

"Fuck... yes, please Ma'am, yes... like that..."

"Oh, and if I then do it like this... how's that?"

"Uhmmm... uhhmmm... oh... ohhhhhh... yeah, that really hurts Ma'am...!"

"I know, but good or bad? You have to tell me..."

"Oh... oh... good, yes, good... ohhh... ummm... ugh... yes, good..."

"Harder boy? Tell me if you want it harder..."

"Uummm... no, no harder...NO! I said NOO! FUCK!!!"

A laugh. "Too much, boy?"

"Ugh... uhmmm... yes... oh... no... no, not too much... almost too much... ooohhhhh... god!... good... ughhhh... jesus!"

"Okay, what if I do this... this soft nice... on top... good?"

"............"

"Talk to me boy... this now... yes?"

"Yes Ma'am... yes yes yesyesyes... ughhhh... ohhhh... yes..."

"Had enough? Want me to stop?"

"No no please...no please, don't stop... if you want to go harder Ma'am... please... please..."

"Okay... here? Like this...? God, you are loving that aren't you?"

"Yesyesyes... ohhhh... yes... good, just like that..."

"God, you are so fucking beautiful like this... here, if I do this now? There...? You sure?"

"Ohh, god, yes, please pleasepleaseplease..."

"... and harder, you can take it for me can't you boy?"

"Yes yes Ma'am, I can, I can... please..."

Tethered

I am exhausted, can barely keep my eyes open, lying under the sheet, waiting for sleep to take me. I shift a little to the edge of the bed and reach down. My fingers find skin and I travel it lightly, orientating myself to you. I hear you shift as you turn your face up to me, and my fingertips touch your hair, forehead, eyes behind eyelids flickering at my touch, your lashes heavy and thick, even in the dark. My fingertips smooth over your cheek, and I touch your lips, soft soft soft and I stroke them, so soft. I push just a little and your mouth opens for me. I can hear you breathing, as I slide two fingers into your wetness. Your lips close around them and you suck gently, your tongue a soft lapping.

And oh, god, it immediately makes me wet, your mouth and your tongue and your lips, and I feel my heartbeat quicken and my breathing into the darkness gets heavy and shallow. I close my eyes, so tired, and let your mouth become distant, like a dream of a mouth, and I feel myself drift away, knowing you are there, tethered by the side of my bed, my fingers in your mouth and I wonder if you will sleep.

I FEEL LIKE KISSING

I feel like kissing, which is something I adore, and which I am missing already even though I made the boy give me his mouth before he left because it makes him weak, and I love when he is like that. My mouth is tender still, my lips feel swollen, his taste is still on my tongue and I just can't get enough of his mouth.

Kissing is like great sex without the sex, the promise of sex, and sometimes better than sex, and every aspect of sex can be put into it, and every aspect of D/s can be expressed in it, and I get to be soft and tender and harsh and hard, and I get to hurt and bite and put him where I want with a fist in his hair and I get to tease and penetrate and force and play and taste him from the inside.

Kissing is completely, utterly and hugely underrated. It is like an obsession for me, kissing, oh, and mouths, god, mouths are just incredibly beautiful and tactile and soft and wet and mobile and expressive and altogether delicious.

I feel like kissing.

Breaking you

My head is full of you and my pussy wet with you, fucking you, helpless and crying on that beach, and you are so thin, and in pain, with pieces of you missing because I have taken them and swallowed them. And yes, my fingers in your mouth to turn your head to me, and I want to kiss you, but I can't reach your mouth no matter how far I twist your head towards me and I want to shove my fingers into your throat and see you struggle.

And it hurts you, the fucking and the contact, because your skin is raw and flayed open and still you fuck me back, and this thing, my cock, is hitting my clit every time I thrust into you so I don't care how much it hurts you.

And my fingers around your neck then, tightening, and you are having trouble breathing, and you are crying, and beautiful. And I don't cut you, and I don't squeeze the life out of you, but I know I will, and you are scared, and your body is so fragile and I feel like I am breaking you with the fucking and I can't think about anything except coming, until I come.

I love...

I love talking with you.

I love hearing about what you are doing.

I love when you speak nonsense to me.

I love that you make me laugh.

I love how your voice gets lower and softer and more beautiful when you talk about your body and describe to me your bruises and cuts.

I love how that feels like seduction to me.

I love that they belong to me, those marks.

I love how you breathe, heavy and rasping when you are about to come, or not allowed to come.

I love how you ask me if I want to hurt you, please.

I love that desperate sucking of breath you do when you are dealing with pain.

I love how you make those soft grunting sounds.

I love how you say my name in that way.

I feel the lust rise from the pit of my stomach even as I write all that, relentlessly turning over and hitting me deep inside. I want more of you, I always want more of you, I want to make you do that over and over until you can't bear it anymore.

Crash

I am already crashing up against him on the way home, seeking impact. He sees the aggression before we get inside, he probably saw it building hours before, and fed it quietly all night long... slipping scraps under the table into the hungry maw when I wasn't looking. We are still giggling and being silly as I push him police-style into the apartment.

"Only cuts and bruises, no permanent damage please!" he says.

He makes me laugh.

I am bristling with pent up energy that spikes as he closes the door, he softens under it. It looks like he is still moving around being normal, hanging coats, getting a drink, chatting, but it is clear as day to me.

He is suddenly underwater, every movement slows as he makes himself open, accessible. It is imperceptible, subtle, it screams at me like a siren, he may as well rip open his chest and bleed all over the floor for the effect it has on me.

God, I love how he can do this. I don't know how he does it, but he does it and it makes my blood boil. Every act now becomes a superficial irrelevance: he is just waiting in this void, making sure he is within reach of me, being available, signalling vulnerability, waiting.

I don't even know how it happens, details get lost when I am like this.

He is suddenly face down on the bed (clothes, where are his clothes?). I am on him. His wrists quickly attached to the frame, I straddle and claw at him, I am seeking purchase, I am trying to get inside him through his skin. I am having trouble breathing, gasping desperately for air, looking around to find something to get inside him.

I undo my belt quickly, slide it through the loops of my jeans, stand back and swing it through the air at him. It strikes him with a satisfyingly solid feel and sound, a sharp and heavy crack. I hit him again, and again, his back, his arse. He tries to stay still, but manoeuvres himself so he can wrap a protective arm around the back of his neck. I see him protect himself, know that I am not familiar with the length of the belt, and should feel bad, but I don't. The belt flies over and down again and again, each time the sound and force resonates up my arm and into me, his skin reddening. He feels like he is cowering from me, I know he is afraid.

I land on his back with a thump and lean down to him, he peeks up at me and it would normally break my heart, that look. He is hopeful, he seeks reassurance and his mouth opens as he reaches for the kiss that he knows is coming.

I hiss at him, cold and cruel. "You think you get to kiss me, bitch?!"

I see him recoil from the words, he doesn't know what the right answer is. His brain stutters.

I slap him, it is awkward in that position, he winces, his eyes screwed shut, the face of a boy betrayed, I slap him again, and again, harder, he knows better than to turn away, but I know he is struggling to remain open to me.

"I asked, do you think you get to kiss me, bitch?!"

"I... I had hoped... maybe... I had hoped so... Ma'am..."

I shake my head, and I slap him over and again, trying to get some force behind it. I am reeling, I can't breathe, the room is a vacuum and I am struggling to get air, gasping loudly into the silence, sucking at the emptiness.

He sees that I am scaring myself, hears something close to the edge, it brings him back. He whispers comfort and permission, both.

"It's okay, it's okay, sweetheart..."

It nearly undoes me, that incredible sweetness, I feel myself melting from the inside, then I shake it off and the tenderness between us is gone.

I stand up and turn the belt around, the buckle end hits him, the feel and sound dull and unsatisfying, so I try it again. And again. Blood beads in spots where it cuts him on his arse, his back. I wipe some onto my finger and taste him, it is strangely calming.

I get some more and bring my fingers to his mouth. He licks at them, and I push them into his mouth. He is expecting to taste my pussy, but he gets the iron taste of blood instead, I don't know if he is surprised, I don't care.

I finally step away and look at him, my breathing harsh and rasping, his back rising and falling as if we are keeping time together, his flesh is a bright red bloom, blood leaves dark evidence of violence across his skin. I am not nearly done with him yet.

After the violence

I do these things to you, these violent things, these things that hurt, these things that make you scared and hard and conflicted and they are hot and they make me come and then, when I have come, I want to wrap you up, all arms and legs and skin-softness, safe, and have your mouth, open and tender and gentle and I want to kiss you better and whisper sweet things to you, into your mouth, and be sweet and protective with you.

And sometimes, sometimes, that scares you more than the other, doesn't it?

Holding back

She led him back to the bed, still blindfolded, and made him get on it, lying in the centre, face up.

She attached his cuffed wrists to the corners of the bed, sliding her naked body across him, leaning on him, enjoying the feel of his skin under hers. She moved down his body and put ankle cuffs on him, spreading his legs wide, attaching them to the ropes at the bottom of the bed. When he was spreadeagled and bound, she sat back and looked at him. He looked incredible; lean-muscled, strong, vulnerable, sightless, helpless. And his cock was beautiful, not a word she generally applied to cocks, but there it was; hard, perfect, beautiful.

She slid her body up his, tender, stroking him with her breasts, her stomach, her thighs, his body reaching for more of her. He knew, knew, that she would want to kiss him, and she saw him anticipate her with his mouth and she moaned silently deep in her throat at his gently opening lips, his face tilting up to her.

Instead, though, she touched his skin elsewhere with her mouth, not even tasting, just touching her lips to him, his pale nipples, the outline of his ribs, his navel, his ridged stomach, the hollows at his hips, taking her time, soft. She lifted her mouth from him and suddenly licked his cock hard from base to head and he grunted in surprise and pleasure, his body involuntarily arching up to her. She looked quickly up into his face. His mouth was open, his neck tensed, a grimace on his face. She pressed her pussy against his leg, her wetness against his skin. She licked his cock once more and let his reaction wash over and into her. She wanted to growl and bite and scratch and mark him, but held herself back and was terrifyingly, frustratingly gentle with him.

She smiled, unseen by him.

Now this... this was going to be fun.

Kissing you awake

You are sleeping now, finally, and twitchy, restless. Are you dreaming, or are your thoughts silent and is it only your body imagining your life outside of sleep?

I watch your face, so soft in repose, innocent and beautiful, an occasional frown creasing your forehead. I would like to wake you gently, to see how long it would take for your mind to register that there are lips on yours, softly nudging, until you start to feel it in your half sleep and unconsciously open your mouth to me, not even knowing what is going on.

And I like this sleepy, half awake boy who just kisses whoever's mouth he finds on his, and opens himself up and makes some low sound when the kissing makes his cock wake up.

I just want to make out, and I never use the term 'make out', but I do like it. Or the term 'pash' is equally good. Both are adolescent and perfect.

I could wake you slowly like that and we could pash.

No rules

She looks at him.

"I'm so sorry Ma'am," he says again, contrition written on his face.

"Did you forget, or did you just decide it wasn't important?" she asks.

"I just didn't... think of it... I forgot Ma'am..." He knows his answer is inadequate.

"I see."

"I have no excuse, I'm truly sorry Ma'am."

"How many rules do you have? How many things do I ask for, boy?"

"Five Ma'am, there are only five."

"Do you think that's unreasonable? Do you think that's too much for you?"

"No! No Ma'am... I just... I just fucked up... please..."

"Do I have to remind you every single time? Is that it? Really?"

"No Ma'am... I will do better, I have no excuse, I'm so sorry..."

"Right... well since you can't follow the rules, I am revoking all of them for the next half hour. You will be a submissive without rules. You will not call me

Ma'am, you will not show me any particular respect, you are free to do whatever you want. No rules. Do you understand?"

His face shows his confusion.

"Yes Ma'a... Yes. Very unexpected, but crystal clear." He looks relieved at the punishment.

"You have my name written on your body: Go now and scrub it off."

His face drops, but he knows better than to argue. "Okay..."

He trudges off to the bathroom. When he returns he has his hand under his shirt, and she knows his fingers are touching the redness where he has scrubbed her name off his skin. He looks pathetic.

They sit and talk for a while, about an upcoming wedding, about plans for the weekend. She watches him, knows he is uncomfortable. He is looking more and more miserable.

Finally she says, "How does this feel? To have no rules?"

"It's horrible..."

"You thought it was a trivial punishment, a welcome respite... that it was going to be easy?"

He nods. "I was confused at first, then the penny dropped and I felt sick, it makes me feel sick... I understand the punishment, it's a good one."

"What is it?"

"To find out what it's like when you don't care what I do, to just do whatever I want, to feel as if I'm not your submissive. I miss being under your control already, I feel lost…"

She nods. "I want you to understand what happens if you don't follow the rules: It doesn't work does it?"

He shakes his head, his eyes downcast. "No, it really doesn't."

She looks at her watch. "Okay, the half hour is up. The punishment is over, boy."

He smiles broadly, relief written on his face. She smiles back at him.

He drops to his knees and looks up at her. "Thank you Ma'am."

She beckons him close, and writes her name back on his skin to claim him, to bring him home. She feels his pleasure at being back in his place.

"I really missed your rules a lot, even just for half an hour. I know that sounds kind of stupid. I *like* having them: They remind me who I am, they remind me that I'm yours, Ma'am."

She cocks her head at him and traces her name written on his skin with her fingertip.

"I know," she replies.

She cups his chin and lifts his face to hers, leaning down to hold his gaze.

"… and yes, you're mine."

Offering

I smell like sex when I leave you, a low musky scent, and if I can smell my own wetness, I have to think I am walking around with pheromones bleeding out of my pores, floating around me like big neon signs that flash 'in heat, come and get me'. I feel like I have a hunger written on my face, and every man I see looks like prey, and they know they do and either return my gaze with a question or quickly avert their eyes.

And I am thinking about you as I eye off other men, my head swimming with images of you, cut and bleeding on your knees, covered in bruises, hard and wanting more, looking up at me and whispering "please pleaseplease", and I want to give you more, I want you to take more and I want you to fall from your knees onto the floor with it, until your 'please' turns into 'please no', until I hear desperation and struggle and an edge of panic.

And I know you will give me that, I know you will offer me your obliteration.

You'll offer me everything, won't you baby?

THINGS I AM NOT DOING TO YOU

We are lying face to face in bed; you are naked, I am dressed. I am touching you, stroking you gently, my face close to yours, and I am talking to you about what you really want me to do rather than this gentle petting of your face, your arms, your nipples, your stomach, your cock and you are watching my lips move as I talk and I am watching you watching.

"You want me to do something hard and rough to you, don't you?"

"Yes... please..."

"Like here, at your nipples, you would like it if I pinched them really hard, and pulled at them, and dug my nails into them, wouldn't you, instead of just touching them like this?"

"Yes Ma'am..."

"And here, your stomach, you would love it if I pressed a knife hard into you and made lines and letters and carved my name into you with it and made you bleed, instead of this soft tracing of shapes...?"

You moan softly, thinking about it and how much it would hurt.

"Yes... yes, please..."

"And wouldn't you love it if I hit you hard with the knife, here above your cock, instead of playing gently with the hair there like this?"

You nod, breathing heavily into my mouth. "Yes, please Ma'am, please..."

"And here, your cock, you really want me to smack it hard, and sink my teeth into it, instead of just running my fingertips over it like this, don't you?"

You whimper, looking at me. You want it so badly, and some sound comes out of your mouth, a moaning, desperate sound...

You shift towards me, you want to get closer, to get some contact. I shake my head and you come to a halt.

I bring my lips to yours, just barely touching, and I continue to talk to you with my lips on yours, but I don't kiss you, I just whisper to you softly about the things I am not doing to you and I touch you gently.

And eventually I ask if you want me to kiss you and you say, "Yes, yes please..." and you reach for me with your mouth. I pull back from you, out of reach. No, you don't get to kiss me.

I can taste your disappointment, your whole body is thrumming with need, vibrating on some frequency that neither of us quite understand.

I ask you if you want me to stop with this talk and gentle tenderness because you are not getting what you want and your eyes widen and you quickly shake your head and beg me please not to stop whispering to you or touching you and your desperation is in your stomach and in your throat and in your cock and in your mouth and you feel like you will explode with it.

And fuck, seeing you like this and listening to you like this and not giving you what you want is incredibly hot and makes me slip my hand down into my jeans and play my fingers over my clit, all the while whispering to you about the things I am not doing to you, and it makes me moan against your lips and you suck my breath as if you can taste me in it and your body is trembling and I know you are aching, and the knowing and the needy desperation and my fingers around and inside me make me come.

Coming when you are not coming

It's been twelve days since you were allowed to come.

You have never felt closer to me, you have never been more beautiful.

I come over you not coming for me, and then I come again. I come over how much you want to come. I come over you thanking me for not letting you come. I come over you getting hard for me over and again. I come over you nearly coming and struggling to stop yourself. I come over your newly found sensitivity. I come over telling you how not letting you come makes me come. I come over listening to you in pain and how that brings you close to coming. I come over hearing you whisper, "God, I want to come... oh please..." I come over you nearly coming before you are even fully hard. I come over you not being able to be touched when you are so hard it hurts. I come over bringing you to the edge and not letting you come over and over. I come over telling you things that make you want to come. I come over thinking up tortures that will make it harder for you to not come. I come over that desperate sound you make when you are trying not to come.

I want to come for every second that you are not coming.

I haven't told you how many more days, but I know you are thinking it's at least six more. Six more you can deal with.

But what if it's six more after that, and six more after that?

I know what you mean

You say to me "Please, Ma'am," and I know what you mean.

You mean "Hit me hardest now, I want to be bruised and battered and sorry-sore for ages afterward, so make it count please Ma'am, and I can take it pretty hard, don't hold back, and then please during or after or before, please kiss me and let me beg for you to kiss me because I want my mouth to feel your mouth both tender and aggressive-hard and desperate, kissing until I can't breathe with want and my mouth is aching and all of me is aching, and I want to feel the shadow of it afterwards, for ages afterwards, moving my body around and feeling the pain in it and touching my lips and tasting those kisses."

You say to me "Please, Ma'am," and I know what you mean.

THIS KISS

"Kneel," I say, and my stomach lurches with lust as you immediately drop to your knees, your hands still clasped behind your head.

I tilt your chin up, lean down and bring your mouth to me, touching your lips softly with mine, nudging your mouth open. I hold back a moan in my throat as you aggressively reach up for more, your tongue entering my mouth, and I return your kiss hard, pulling your mouth tighter against mine with a fist in your hair.

We stay there, locked in this never ending kiss that reaches straight into my core and twists it into knots, this kiss whose silent tongues speak of desperation and need and desire and oblivion, this kiss that makes me want to push you back onto the floor and fuck your mouth with my cunt right there, this kiss that I can't bear to let go of, this kiss that makes me completely lost.

I pull away from you at long last and catch my breath, drinking in the sight of you, naked and kneeling and hard, your eyes on mine, your mouth slightly open, your lips soft and full, your breathing loud and deep. I touch your lips with my fingers and you close your eyes and open your mouth to me. Your automatic reaction makes my heart skip a beat, and I slip a finger into your waiting mouth and feel your lips close around it, a sucking, your tongue lapping at it. I feel you pulling my finger into your mouth and all I can think about is what went before, my head spinning with it, my mouth tingling with loss and want.

I reach down to you for more of the kiss, I have missed it in the few minutes I have been away from it and I sigh with pleasure when I guide your mouth back to mine and bring it back to life. This is one of the things you were born for, this kiss, this kiss that should go on forever, this kiss that makes everything in me flow like liquid, this kiss that offers me your soul through your mouth.

Convince Me

On the floor, hands cuffed, you are cowed, and hurt, and scared. And I am standing over you calling you a fucking bitch and a dirty slut and I have a strap-on that I am forcing into your mouth and down your throat, listening to you gag, with my hand on the back of your head to pull you further onto it, and I know it hurts your mouth, your throat and I hiss at you to look up at me while you choke around it and struggle to breathe and I shove it further down your throat and you try to look up into my face, and you are gagging and that pushes the base against my clit so I shove harder against you.

I pull your mouth off my cock so I can slap your face and I make you look up at me after each slap and say "Thank you Ma'am," and I do it over and over until your cheek is bright red and you come back to me slower and slower, which makes me mad, your slowness, and makes me want to hit you harder, so I do, before I shove my cock back down your throat.

And you keep your mouth open for my cock, saliva running out of the corners because you can't swallow and I am both shoving into you and pulling your head onto my cock.

"Look up at me, you filthy slut."

And you do and I want to hit you more, all over, and hard.

So I shove you backwards away from me and you nearly fall over.

"Crawl and get me the fucking belt, bring it to me in your mouth, bitch."

And you crawl on all fours and it makes me want to fuck you, watching you crawl.

You bring me the belt in your bruised mouth, your breathing is heavy, and you kneel up to me and wait. I know you want this, so I make you beg me to hurt you. Not some half arsed compliant begging because I say so, but real heartfelt begging and if it's not convincing, we will stop right here boy, right now, so fucking beg.

You beg, over and over you beg for me please, please to hurt you. And it's not good enough, so do it right, you need to convince me to do it.

I shove my cock into your mouth while you are begging, right down the back of your throat and hold your nose and stop there until you start to struggle to breathe. Then I pull out, and you gasp for air, sucking desperate breaths.

I say, "I don't believe you boy, beg me."

And you are trying to breathe and trying to beg and I do it again, shoving my cock into the back of your throat, holding your nose, struggle, release, beg me... and again, and again...

"I still don't believe you boy, now beg me..."

Scent marking

I wonder if you can smell me in your sleep, colouring your thoughts and invading your dreams. I have marked you with my scent, putting it on your skin, your lips, reminding you that I am here, reminding you who you belong to.

I like having you smell of me, walking around in the world like a shadow of me, wafting around you as you go about your day, a hint of me touching you unexpectedly when you turn back on yourself.

I like having you smell me also, and I know you bring the scent to your nose when you want to feel close and I feel you breathe in deeply, sucking me into your lungs to bring and keep me there, touching every cell, unwilling to let the air back out, trying to taste the scent on your tongue and all the way to the back of your throat and inside you.

I wonder if you can smell me in your sleep and in your wakeful moments and when you aren't paying attention and when you are and when you see something that makes you think of me and when you see nothing and are thinking of me.

Have I marked you with my scent enough so that you just smell me, anyway and always?

Sex-noise

There is noise in your head, I can hear it from here, a humming, making your body ache, drawing a moaning sound from deep in your throat, a spinning, floaty, throbbing sex-noise that makes you dreamy and hard and desperate, that makes your eyes glassy and your mouth wet with want.

I whisper, "Are you paying attention boy?"

"Yes Ma'am, I'm paying attention..."

I can barely hear you.

Sharper, no louder, I bring you back to me.

"Are you paying attention boy?"

A soft beautiful moan, a focussing... you breathe, "Yes Ma'am" and I feel it go straight to my cunt.

I am already thinking about what I want from you next.

BEST LAID PLANS

I am not planning to play with you, I am planning to put you to bed and leave you to sleep. I've said goodnight already when I tell you to take off your clothes: I am just going to put you to bed and go. I tell you as much.

"Yes Ma'am," you say.

As they come off, your shirt, your jeans, I start to kick in, feel my heart start to thump in my chest, my stomach lurching with lust.

I want something from you, I always want something from you.

I start with a permanent marker, making your cock hard, writing my name on it, it's mine, I own it, my cock.

"Whose cock is it?" I ask you, unnecessarily.

"It's your cock Ma'am."

"It belongs to me."

You nod. "It belongs to you Ma'am."

I want to write my name on every part of you, across your chest and your nipples, on your ribs, around your navel, along the flat of your stomach, against the bones of your hips, across the muscles of your thighs, over your knees, along the swell of your calves, on the soles of your feet, around the curves of your arse, into the small of your back, across your shoulder blades, into the nape of your neck, I want to mark all of you as mine.

Instead, I choose your left hip, 'beautiful' goes there. Then your right hip, 'boy bitch'.

"Beautiful boy bitch," I whisper to you.

My lace panties go into your mouth, you make a muffled sound as they hit the back of your throat. Soft touches of your claimed cock while I whisper to you about fucking and violence and passing you around like a piece of meat.

Your heavying breaths, your fuck-me moans, your quickening grunts into my panties and into my ear make my heart rise into my throat.

You are close to coming when I stop, stop stop stopstop, pull my panties out of your mouth so that I can hear your heavy desperate breaths.

"Beautiful boy bitch, beautiful boy bitch, beautiful boy bitch with my cock..." I whisper obsessively. "What are you? Say it."

"I'm a beautiful boy bitch with your cock," you whisper in my ear in your soft porn voice.

"Say it again," I tell you.

"Beautiful boy bitch with your cock," you draw out the words because you know I love that.

"Again."

"Beautiful boy bitch with your cock," your voice lower now as I make a sound of pleasure.

I make you say it again and again, and then again, your voice making a link straight to my cunt.

I stay with you a little longer, finally putting you to bed... really now, I am just going to put you to bed and leave you to sleep...

Greedy slut

She stands before him, looking into his tear stained face, his eyes brimming. He holds her gaze and she sees his adoration, his surrender in them, and she has never loved him more. She brings her face to his and licks the tears she has caused from his cheeks, kisses his mouth softly, tenderly, feeling his tongue tentatively reach for hers. She sighs into his mouth with pleasure.

As he watches, she slowly takes off her panties. She holds the wetness to his lips, he can smell her, his tongue already licking at it, trying to suck it into his mouth.

She laughs softly. "Greedy slut."

She shoves her panties hard into his mouth, down into the back of his throat, he tries not to gag, making a coughing sound.

She runs her palm across his inflamed arse, and feels him twitch.

"Every time you sit or move I want you to think of me," she whispers.

He already does. He hardly breathes without thinking of her.

She walks behind him again, reaches around his chest and pulls him into her body from the back grinding against his burning arse, reaching around him to torture his nipples. Pinching, pulling, twisting until he moans and squirms, trying desperately to push back harder against her, to increase the contact. She feels his desperation as he tries to fight his restraints.

She reaches for his cock, and strokes it, just once, hard, and is rewarded with a groan as he tries to thrust against her fingers. She swipes the pre-come at the end of his cock onto her fingers and smears it around his lips.

"Lick it clean, boy," she whispers, and watches as he tries to comply, her panties in his mouth preventing him from bringing his tongue to his lips. He shakes his head, his brow furrowed, he grunts at her softly. She thinks she hears "I'm sorry Ma'am."

She pushes up against him and slips his cock between her legs.

"Can you feel how wet you make me?" she whispers as she rubs herself against him.

He can barely nod, he groans into the panties, the sensation is so good.

She rocks her hips back and forth stroking her clit with his cock, reaching up to him, offering her mouth. He leans down to her, the panties in his throat stop him from kissing her, but still he moves hopefully to her mouth, she can hardly breathe, panting into his mouth, concentrating on her clit rubbing against him.

She hangs onto him as she quickens her pace, her soft sounds being swallowed by his mouth. She leans back a little so she can reach his nipples, pinching and twisting them hard enough to make him wince with a sharp intake of breath, his hips thrust forward, fucking against her, he pulls against the cuffs, he is moaning into his gag. She suddenly steps back from him, both of them breathing heavily.

She holds his gaze, catching her breath, she half smiles, he tilts his head, his chest heaving, his look a questioning. She leans down to his nipples, this time with her mouth, her teeth sinking into his flesh and pulling at them, he gasps. She strokes his cock gently with her fingertips, just enough to be frustrating and she is rewarded with a groan and feels him tensing to get more.

She pulls her wet panties out of his mouth, grabs his face and pulls him to her, kissing him hard, he strains to get more of her tongue, her face, any part of her into his mouth, on his body. He begs with his grunts and moans and the tension in his body, all of him reaching for more of her.

She releases the kiss, undoes the cuffs at his wrists and ankles and he sinks to his knees in front of her.

She walks away from him to the corner armchair, and calls him to her.

"Here, boy."

He crawls to her, kneels at her feet and waits. He feels her hand in his hair, she pulls his head up to her, he looks her in the eye and runs his tongue around his lips. She smiles, he is teasing her.

She slowly widens her knees and directs his face to her pussy. He moans softly and reaches for her, his mouth slightly open, his tongue out, he can smell her. She holds his face inches from her.

"Lick me, baby," she whispers.

He reaches forward with his tongue, just touching her wetness, straining against her fist in his hair holding him back. He groans in frustration, pulling against her grip in his hair.

"Please Ma'am, please."

She holds fast for what feels like forever, feeling him pulling as hard as he can to get his mouth on her.

She finally relents and releases the pressure, and his lips and tongue are immediately on her and it's soft, hard, rough, sweet, perfect and she thrusts into his mouth, against his tongue and his hands are under her arse holding her into his mouth and she is lost and it goes on forever.

When she comes she arches almost out of the chair, crying out, obsessively repeating a moaning.

"Oh oh oh ohhh..."

He moves with her, keeping her cunt hard against his mouth, and he keeps licking until the waves are finished and even after that and she has to force his face from her.

She lies back, her hand in his hair, she catches her breath, holding his face against her thigh, she pets him absently.

Sweet things

She catches her breath and leans down to kiss him, tasting herself on him, he closes his eyes to accept her kiss, tender and soft, she holds his mouth to hers and speaks to him in the feather light, never ending kiss. She smiles when she sees his cock, still hard and she strokes his face and brings his head to lay in her lap, and runs her fingers through his hair, petting him gently.

She wants to whisper sweet things to him, to whisper thank you, to whisper of tenderness, to whisper of her heart aching, to whisper how beautiful he is, to whisper how she adores him, but she whispers none of those things and pets him softly.

Men in kilts

He is wearing a flirty leather mini-kilt, a white shirt and patent black Doc Martins. I watch him from across the space as he flogs a woman tied to a cross, his skirt flicking up in the most gorgeous manner. He has strong, shapely legs and the most amazing flogging style: almost taking running start, putting his whole body into it, beautiful to watch.

Afterwards, we lock eyes, we talk, flirt. I watch his mouth move as he speaks to me and imagine what he would taste like. He nods at the rack and smiles at me, a question in his eyes. We have a power struggle, laughing. He wants to flog me, I want to flog him... damn switches!

I step close and start to undo his shirt, my eyes on his face. He allows it, decision made. I tell him softly about safe words, tell him gently what I am planning to do to him as I touch his skin under his shirt.

"Tell me if you have a problem with any of that, won't you?" I say.

I give a come-hither nod to my girlfriend. She saunters over, smirking.

"You want a piece of this?" I ask her, gesturing at him.

She looks him up and down and nods. "Oh yeah."

I raise an eyebrow at him. He smiles at me.

"No problem," he says. "Don't go easy on me will you?"

He makes me laugh.

I bend him over the rack and cuff his wrists, kicking his legs apart.

I start off on his back with a flogger while she circles, playing around him. I warm up on him and start to apply some pressure, he resists me, being stoic, which irritates me. I put more force into it to try and get a reaction, but I am not getting what I want from him. He is silent, still. I try different implements, different spots, different kinds of sensations... nothing. Finally I nod to my girlfriend and hold up the flogger. She gives me a big smile, and takes it from me.

I bend down in front of him, caress his face, grip his hair in my fist to lift his face to mine, stroking his cheek with mine, breathing in his ear, whispering to him, biting at his ear lobe. She is going hard at his back now and I reach under the rack and pinch and squeeze at his nipples, watching his face, he has one pierced and I pull at it. He fights me still, refusing to give it up and really let go. I am rougher on his nipples and chest when she is flogging him harder, keeping pace with her. I bend over him, his face to my breasts, to scratch and stroke down his back when the whipping stops or slows.

I hold my mouth to his, breathing on his lips. He

refuses to reach to kiss me, I refuse to give him the kiss. Frustrating for both of us, neither willing to give in.

Afterwards, we talk a little, I leave him in the care of my girlfriend. I am disappointed with how it went. Sometimes I can't get the exchange, the heat, the reactions that I want from a boy.

I am watching another scene when he finds me. Without a word, he slips an arm tight around my waist, slides a hand into my hair, he pulls my mouth to his and kisses me, a violent, hot, hard, hungry kiss. I wrap my arm around his head, pull him against me, push my hips into him and bite at his lips, hard, feral and I hang on to his head, holding him there as he tries to jerk away from my teeth. I feel his cock jump against me. I think I may have drawn blood. He pulls back and looks accusingly at me, hurt, touching his fingers to his lips.

"That fucking hurt!"

I eye his crotch. "You loved it," I state. It's a simple fact.

He smiles, still fingering his lip.

"Maybe," he says, tilting his head. "I owe you one..." he adds.

I laugh. "Yeah good luck with that."

I smack him on the arse as he turns to leave, he swats me back.

SINGLE MINDED PASSION

I miss you with a single minded passion, though I have only just seen you and then been asleep, and today I promised myself that I would do some copious amounts of work because you won't be here and instead I am thinking about you and wanting so to get on the phone and talk to you and call you horrible filthy names and whisper to you about violent rape and fuckery with your face in the dirt in the middle of nowhere and I don't want anyone else on you or to have you right now and I just want to make you tell me over and over with every part of you, one by one that it belongs to me until we have covered every piece (who does this cock belong to... who do those lips belong to... whose tongue is that, stick it out... who does that dirty slutty fuckhole of a mouth belong to...), but in my head they are still there, the others, wanting to get at you like I have no control over them, they who are me, who want to shove their cocks into your mouth, always with the cocks, and they line up to get into your mouth, each one who is fucking your mouth telling the others, who can hardly wait, what your mouth feels like, wet, your mouth gets wet and hot and I can feel the back of your throat closing when you gag, and you are tied down, kneeling, awkward, with your back against a tree, your wrists pulled back around the trunk, and rough bark scrapes your back raw as your head smashes into it over and over with this cock being shoved into your mouth, only coming out when I want to step back and smash your face, and the others who are waiting are giving instructions, egging on the one who has you at the moment, 'fucking smack the little bitch!', 'fuck his face harder, make him take it all', 'choke the filthy slut, make him pass out and then fuck him!', 'when do we get his ass, fuck this, bet he's like some tight little cunt back there', 'just fucking move him so we can get in his arse' and one of them holds up a branch, rough and too wide 'let's fuck him with this, see how the dirty bitch likes that' and they all laugh, but you can see that they really want to do that. And boots are kicking at your legs, shoving them apart, they are already thinking about your arse, your face still being fucked, and you are trying to do what I want, trying to suck my cock, and I keep pulling your head onto me just so that I can shove harder back against your face and make your head smash back into the tree and you are grunting around my cock each time and your nose and eyes are running, and then I have to step out somehow and watch the violence of these men who are me because they untie you and they invite you to run, you are already weak and hurt and so fucking scared and I want to rescue you, I want to kiss you and take you to the ground and get as much of my skin on yours as I can get, to cover you with my body, your cock hard between our bodies, my stomach on yours, my breasts against your chest, eating up your mouth, and feel you open up to me with one scared eye on them and your raw skin rubbing against the ground, and they know that I want your arse, this arse that I own, and they hold your legs up and apart for me and I shove my cock into your arse and fuck you and you sob into my mouth because it's so fucking good and it's me-and-you and it hurts your arse and it rips more skin off your back, and they can watch and they can want your mouth and your arse, but both are mine, and fucking you and touching you and kissing you and having those sounds go straight into my mouth, all that makes me want to hurt you and then we come back to the violence, and I don't want to stop fucking you, I just want to come, I want your mouth on my cunt, and your tongue and your lips on me, but it's too gentle and I step out, and they invite you to run.

Your voice

I love your voice... I just love it.

You have a perfect voice for sex, for play, for pain, for desperate need, for begging, for breathing my name, it is so so beautiful and I love how you talk to me and I love how you say Ma'am and I love how you murmur to yourself and I love that every strike makes you gasp or groan and I love the way you breathe, heavy and loud and I love how you swear and I love how you repeat my words back at me and I love how you tell me what you are thinking about... all of it, it's so fucking sexy.

I have your voice in my head and listen to it like audio-porn over and over and there is something in it that makes me feel like I am melting from the inside and opening up, like my stomach is going to cave in because everything inside is now like molten lava, and that liquid is going to pour out of my cunt, like a lurch that has turned to God and can no longer punch me.

Domme-space

My vision closes in until there is only him. There is nothing else, only me and him.

Time slows down.

It feels like my heart is going to burst out of my chest, and joy and lust rise like a wave from there. I feel like I am not even consciously thinking anymore, just feeling and doing: it is completely instinctual, like my essence knows what I want even though my mind is so high it isn't really engaging.

If I get into this space, there is no way I would interrupt it for anything. He becomes a tool to feed this energy. I will never feel a connection or a love as strongly as I do at that time. I also never feel *his* place in relation to me more strongly. He is wholly mine in this.

It is intense and powerful, and the hyper-focus in it leaves no room for anything else. We are in it together and everything else becomes meaningless. Sound, vision, sensation, energy, all concentrated into the space between us. Every nuance is a blaring siren, clear and loud. It feels like I can see every hair on his body react, hear the blood pumping through his veins, smell the single bead of sweat gathering on his upper lip.

There is nothing like it.

And perhaps hours later, spent and sated, I come out of it, and down from it. Trying to hang onto it for as long as possible before surfacing.

Each delicate spider-web strand of connection breaks slowly in the aftermath, sadly floating away until it dissipates and the world returns.

Day 31 of chastity

Oh god, and with my heart racing and whispering "Oh jesus" to you and my stomach lifted into my chest, you are so fucking hot, which is not the right word, but my brain isn't firing.

My wet panties in your mouth and against your cock are filling my head and I whisper to you "Oh" with that catch, that one that is not even a sound.

Desire on my tongue, throbbing relentlessly when you're nearly coming, and not coming, nearly coming, and not coming, over and again.

A thumping heart beats fast in the back of my throat. The wanting makes me so wet I can taste myself in the air.

It makes my fingers ache, my mouth tender.

Fun of hurting

He has been drinking, is verbally flailing around, trying to find purchase.

"What is the fun of hurting me? ... That is the most right question I have ever asked!" he says finally.

"The fun of hurting you is in your reactions, in how it makes you more beautiful, in how it brings out who you are, in the sounds you make in it, in the way you speak to me in the middle of it, in how it makes me wet. It reaches into you and exposes you to me. And that is incredibly hugely mind-blowingly hot."

He looks at me, contemplating my answer. He smiles slowly, shyly.

"Yes Ma'am, and thank you," he says, satisfied with my answer.

I smile back at him.

"Yes boy, and you're welcome."

Snippets

I have been thinking about this afternoon since I left you, scooting home with you in my mind, still incredibly wet, with snippets of you whipping around my head.

I can't even grasp them or make sense of any of them, they just whirl around like a porn reel and I wish I could record and keep it all to replay you again and again.

In pain with a knife against your cock (your cock, that belongs to me, my cock), torture against your nipples, your laugh, both small and shy and louder and open, that humming moan that I so love, you saying Ma'am to me and how easily it falls out of your mouth, your breath in my ear, getting heavy and low, your gagging and that silence that precedes it, those silly conversations in there that I adore, your cock, my cock getting hard when I talk 'that way' to you, soft and low, your asking 'please, please please', my panties being there with you and on you even now while you are sleeping, my wetness on your lips and on your tongue and how you sound, how you sound, how you sound when your breathing gets, like my cock, heavy and hard and every breath is a lurch that goes straight to my cunt, and I feel like I have already forgotten what that sounds like, when you talk to me and react to me, and you echoing my counting of strokes or hits between your soft moaning breaths.

All of it in my head like a tumultuous storm all loud and stunning and there it stays even after I come and I want to come again over it and I feel like it is disappearing already.

That is all

I have used my mouth and hands on your body, and that is all, and you are sore and bruised and hurt and scared and I love the way you look at me through hooded eyes, exposed and open and wanting.

"Are you okay, baby?"

I will ask you a million times before this is over.

"I am okay Ma'am, I promise."

Tearing at your skin

I throw you face-first against the wall and your head hits it with a thud. You are bigger, taller, stronger… we both know it, but this, this violence, this assault makes you weak, makes your knees buckle, makes you struggle to breathe, struggle to stand.

You slump against the wall and I hold you up with an arm around your neck, the other around your chest as my teeth sink into your flesh. Your gasp and moan of pain hits me like a sledgehammer and my sharp rasping teeth close on your skin.

Your hands grab at the wall for purchase, to stop you slipping. I feel your weight in my arms and shove you harder against the unforgiving surface, my hip against your arse forcing you further forward, my grip around your neck tightening.

Your breaths come hard and fast. I bite you relentlessly, thrusting up against you from behind. Every new attack makes you wince and moan, but still you push back against me until I am fucking you against the wall, tearing at your skin like I am going to devour you.

Your head hits the wall again and my mouth finds another spot and digs in.

Surrender

What I love is not the acts, though I love them too.

I love it when I kiss you and you get that look on your face, like you are sinking into it, and you bow your head and you start to look lost, and you make tiny sounds of surrender and your breathing changes and I know you are waiting for me, opening up to me and I fucking love that.

It's like watching an invisible mist come down over you, like watching you become awash with it, seeing you blossom into my beautiful boy as it enters you, feeling you exposing your body and your heart and your emotions and offer them up to me.

That is what makes me want to attack you and be tender with you and hurt you and pet you.

That is what makes me want to cry right now.

First meeting

He spotted her first and caught her eye, nodding recognition. She smiled wearily, made her way to him, she looked up at him for the first time.

"Hello." She smiled as she leaned into him.

He smiled shyly back at her, greeting her, offering to take the luggage trolley.

He had warned her before meeting that he didn't think he would be able to look at her directly, he was right, he couldn't. He was nervous, scared, had had trouble getting to the meeting point, had been terrified he would be late, was carrying the fear with him. He cast sidelong glances at her while she looked directly into his face, trying to read him.

She talked to him as they walked. He made her laugh. She asked him questions, practical matters, about subways and airports and transport in general, and he said it, unprompted, in response to a question: "Yes Ma'am." Taking her by surprise.

Then he murmured softly, "That was easy…"

She looked at him. "Was it?"

He smiled shyly and met her gaze. "Yes Ma'am, it was."

She melted just a little.

It wasn't until they were on the subway that she touched him deliberately, her hand going to the back of his neck, squeezing gently, massaging his skin, she heard his breathing deepen. He leaned forward to give her better access to him, and he stayed in that position, head bowed, stop after stop as she stroked his neck, petted his hair.

She heard him make a soft sound as he sank into her touch and she knew he was going to be just about perfect.

Scared

"I was scared to death to be suddenly naked in your apartment, yes, scared to be starting, scared that you are so pretty, scared that I might fail you or not be what you want. And I will be scared again and again probably Ma'am, when I am with you."

. . .

I have him stand in the centre of the room, hands clasped behind his head. I walk around him touching him a little. I take my time. He starts to breathe heavily. He is so nervous.

"I'm scared," he whispers to me.

I ignore him. I kick his legs apart, touch his skin under his shirt, his stomach, around his waistband, his chest, my face close to his, rubbing against his cheek. No kissing, I want him to reach for me. I touch his nipples, stroke them gently.

"You want me to hurt them, don't you?"

He nods, shy. "Yes Ma'am."

I start to undo his shirt buttons, very slowly. I'm in his face, studying his mouth, his eyes.

"I'm so scared," he repeats, his breath catching.

I melt a little inside, but say nothing.

My mouth close to his, I breathe into him. He reaches for me. I pull back at first, watch his mouth. I feel the lurch rise from deep in my stomach, the hunger. I lean into him, kiss him gently, just touching my lips to his, rubbing against them, licking softly at his mouth, nudging at him, tasting him for the first time, exploratory, delicious. I part my lips against him, he opens his mouth and lets me in. He tastes sweet.

I remove his shirt and the t-shirt under that, undo his belt. He is uncomfortable, shifting positions. I can feel his cock hard against me when I press up to him. He is tense, his breathing ragged and heavy.

"You're going to wash me," I tell him, thinking it will allay his fear a little.

"Yes Ma'am," he whispers, but his apprehension is still palpable.

I kiss him more deeply, he opens his mouth to me, then I am suddenly wanting more. Violently and hotly pulling his head to me, I grab his hands at the back of his head, my other hand at his throat, and I pull his face down to me, biting and sucking at his mouth, his head in the crook of my neck so he is bent over and below me, awkward. I am hot, hungry for him.

He moans into my mouth, beautiful and desperate. The sound makes me squeeze at his throat, hearing him choke, my mouth over his, my cheek against his nose, stopping him from breathing, grabbing at the flesh of his back, digging my fingernails into him. I am violent against him, I feel him giving in, melting into me, and he makes these beautiful sounds in response and they resonate straight to my cunt.

I finally release him, we are both breathing heavily. I lean into him for a moment, then I walk around with my hands on him, touching his bare skin: soft, smooth, unmarked.

"Take off your pants and boxers," I say.

I hear him start to comply before I leave the room.

It's okay

I hurt you with the belt, and I use familiar words and a familiar tone and it is nothing new but I am tentative and feeling my way and pushing myself to do it, and it is short and should be minor and inconsequential but we both know it's not.

Afterwards, we are both breathing emotion and feeling each other for the fallout.

I am raw and splayed open and it feels like my heart is broken and you watch me softly and that makes me burst like ripeness spilling over from my throat and I am crying.

You gentle me like I am some wild creature that you want to calm and bring to you, whispering "It's okay…. it's okay… it's okay sweetheart…" into my ear and it is unbearably sweet.

I know. I am okay, I will be okay, we will be okay.

Gasping for breath

She knew he would scream, so she brought her panties to his mouth and pushed them in, her fingers shoving the lace into his mouth until it was full.

She started to bite him, sinking her teeth through his flesh, sucking at it, chewing at the skin, creating a pattern on his body. He yelled into the gag, writhing in protest under her assault. When she had made enough marks on his body to please her, she turned her attention elsewhere.

She brought her breast to his mouth, he reached for it even though the best he could do with his mouth full was to brush his lips against her skin. She leaned further against his face, covering his nose with her breast and holding it firm against him. She held his head still and pressed harder against him, at first he just wanted to feel her against his face, but then he was trying to breathe against her skin, trying to suck in air. She held his face close against her, cradling his head into her breast, he started to struggle, shaking his head and still she held him close. His body started to flail, his restrained arms pulling against the ropes, his legs kicking, his body jerking from side to side in an attempt to get free. She finally let him go, he sucked air into his nose, coughing through her panties, she pulled the panties out of his mouth and he convulsed with coughs as he pulled air into his lungs.

She covered his gasping mouth with hers and kissed him. He opened up to her mouth, still sucking for air, but wanting her kiss more than he wanted to breathe, reaching for her, harder and more, always wanting more and she kissed him and swallowed his breaths.

Rain hell

I want to rain hell down on you in a massive attack, a slaughter, a bloodbath, so come here, get your clothes off and get on your knees.

Stroking

We are curled together, my back to his stomach, it is warm and quiet, and maybe he thinks I am asleep. He strokes the side of my body, almost absently, but I know it is not without thought and I know there is a slight fear that I might stop him, that he might not be allowed this unbidden touching.

His touch is gentle, but not tentative or hesitant. Starting at the side of my breast, his fingertips tenderly stroke downwards, over each of my ribs, dipping low at my waist, then slipping up over the rise of my hip. I want to make a sound, but remain silent, motionless.

His touch leaves me, and then again, the roller coaster glide over my curves from the top, the swell, the corrugation, the dip, the rise.

It is so quiet I can hear him breathing, deep and slow. He holds his breath on the stroke and I can feel his thoughts through his fingertips; his sweetness, his affection, his gratefulness, his desire, his fear, all laid bare as his hand slides down my body again. I want to arch into it like a cat, to stretch and luxuriate in it, to reach back and bring his mouth to me, but it is hypnotic and it is his to own and I don't want to break the spell.

I close my eyes and wait for the next stroke, which comes slipping down my skin like silk. I melt into it and I try not to hold my breath as I wait for the next one.

Little Black Dress

He had only ever seen her in jeans, or out of jeans—casual either way. Tonight she wore a little black dress, low at the front, much lower at the back, fitted to her curves, with a flirty little skirt that swung as she walked. She had put on some make up, thigh high stockings, and she couldn't quite decide: fuck-me boots, or strappy stiletto sandals.

She met him at the door, wearing one of each, and let him in. She led him into the bedroom and stood before the mirror. She glanced at him.

"Which do you think?" she asked, looking down at her footwear.

He stared at her in silence, his eyes drinking her in. She felt his reaction before she looked back to him. He had not heard the question, was not looking at her footwear, was not formulating an answer. He stared at her as if he was trying to burn her into his memory, as if he had never seen her before.

She clocked his expression and smiled, preening a little. He looked... awed.

She laughed, and reached over to nudge him.

"You aren't even looking at the shoes! Boots or no?" she asked again.

His eyes slid down her body to her feet.

There was a long pause.

"The sandals make your legs look longer," he finally offered.

She nodded. "Sandals it is then."

He sat before her and she offered her boot into his lap, he undid the zip and slid it off, his hands gliding over her stockinged calves and feet. She pointed to her other sandal on the floor and he slipped it onto her foot, doing up the zip at the heel, touching her ankle gently.

"Ready?" she asked.

"Yes, Ma'am."

Sweetness

What I want with you is sweetness, throat-aching softness, heart melting tenderness.

Skin-to-skin, warm against me (you are always warm), as much of you as I can get pressed to me, legs wrapped up together between and over, shifting to get more contact, to get closer, your arms around me, your fingers stroking my skin. I'm pulling you to me, petting your neck, your hair, holding your face to me, licking at your mouth, your lips, your tongue and holding back for once to taste you over and again as if each time is the first, rocking you against me, back and forth in a hypnotic gentle rhythm as I kiss you, skin sliding against skin, our bodies in synchronised motion, kissing, kissing, kissing.

You are the sweetness.

Pornographic statue

I want to keep you there forever, there on the floor like a piece of art. Face to the ground, my panties in your mouth, my stockings over your face, you are made into a voiceless, faceless thing. Needles through your nipples, your arse in the air, cut and bleeding, inviting attention, blood dripping down your chest, your legs.

You make throaty inarticulate grunting sounds into the gag each time I pay you any attention, any time I pass. I want to keep you there, just like that, until I decide I want something else, until I tell you what I want next.

Like some living pornographic statue that I can slap when I pass, or kick with a boot, or fuck with my fingers, or scratch with my nails, or sink my teeth into, or hit with the cane, or pet whenever I feel like it.

BLATHER

I want to just blather on to you about last night and how amazing you were, and brave (which you always are) and baby, I am so proud of you and you are so beautiful, always, but especially when you do the difficult things, when you struggle, when you are my little bitch, when you are this slutty thing and you are somehow small and open and ready and compliant and helpless and I adore you like that and love that you give me that.

More, baby, I always want more.

More?

He is still tied down, glazed, high and head-spun. I bring the glass to his lips and tip the water into his mouth, his throat undulating as he swallows.

"Do you want some more?" I whisper.

He looks up at me, all trust and soul and broken beauty.

He nods. "Yes Ma'am."

I take a sip and lean down to him, touch my lips to his. He reaches up to kiss me, I open my mouth and let the cool water flow into him.

He utters a little cry. "Oh."

It turns into a moan of pleasure when he realises that I am feeding him from my mouth, he opens up to me.

I feel his whole body reacting to this intimacy, trying to lift off the bed to get closer to me. He swallows greedily, sucking at my mouth for more moisture, to prolong the contact. I pull away when he has it all.

"More?" I ask.

He nods eagerly, his eyes on my lips. "Please..."

I take another sip, he watches me approach and opens his mouth.

Slaps

He was endorphined, wrists cuffed and tied to the bed, his eyes open, but not focussed, though they were directed at her. She touched the places that she had hurt, played with them gently. They were hugely tender and each touch brought forth a moan, his body jerking away from her even though she knew he wanted more.

She looked into his unseeing eyes and delivered a slap to his cheek. His face flew to the side and his eyes returned to hers, focussed, strong, locked, his mouth open. She stared into his eyes, connecting him to her, wanting his mouth again and always. She kept her face impassive, his open and wanting, fast breaths through his mouth making his chest heave. She slapped him again and felt him take it, welcome it, felt it resonate from her hand through her body.

His gaze returned to her and she held it, she knew he wanted more, wondered if he would ask for more. He was silent. She turned away from him and directed her attention elsewhere.

Lick me

Earlier, they had been out at his work function. She in her normal jeans and long sleeved t-shirt, a little make up for the occasion, and a glossy-lipped mouth. Killer heels her indulgence, making her 'the 6'3 blonde'.

She had watched him with his colleagues, nodding pleasant hellos, making nice. She exchanging glances with him, keeping track of his whereabouts when she left his side, chatting absently with strangers. Afterwards, they held hands, ran through the rain (like every clichéd romantic story), had drinks, laughed at the 'he said-she said' autopsy of the evening.

Now though, he is blindfolded and his mouth is on her feet, kissing her toes, drawing them into his mouth, licking at the arch of her foot, pressing his lips into her.

"Kiss me all over," she had said. "Start at my feet."

She lays back and closes her eyes, she feels his mouth move up to her ankle.

Eventually, his gentle mouth moves across her back, his lips making patterns only his mind can see, his tongue touching her skin, to the top of her arse and down further, the only sound his breathing.

He kisses first the skin of her cheeks, unseeing behind the blindfold, kissing the colours of her tattoo, the pale softness, moving slowly to the centre where she feels him hesitate before his mouth trails a path between her cheeks. His mouth finds and kisses sensitive skin that makes her stomach lurch with lust, his tongue licking at her arse and away, and then back again.

She feels as if she raises her hips to him, but isn't sure she has moved, his mouth exploring, tasting, lapping at her, a moan rising in her throat, she wonders if she actually utters it, but she thinks she doesn't. He lingers there at her arse for a long time, heaven-soft and tender, she allows it, relaxing into it, until finally he moves on.

Saying 'no'

You are battered and pathetic and wanting. And crying, always the crying.

And I make you beg me to fuck you.

And I say, "No."

And it makes you scared because you think it means this is over and you beg me to take pieces of you and you beg me to kiss you and you beg me to anchor you to the ground with my body and you beg for something, anything.

And I say, "No."

And it makes me come, the begging, the needing, the wanting and the saying 'no'.

Kiss goodbye

I kiss you goodbye, a quick kiss, I think, and I reach for you, kneeling there beside the bed. I hold your face up to me, licking at your upper lip, dipping my tongue behind it and drawing it into my mouth to lap at it, feeling your tongue chasing mine and opening my mouth wider to take more of you into me.

I am gentle with you for a long time, tender, nudging and tasting you, until I suck your lips, your tongue into my mouth, biting down on them suddenly, nibbling and nipping at them, then sucking hard, trying to swallow them, making it hurt you, like I will pull pieces of you into my mouth and swallow them.

You make a soft moaning sound and I feel you open up for me. I want to take more and I know you want to give it.

I pull at you, force you up and backwards, further backwards, your neck and spine bent awkwardly over my knees, and I hold you there, arched, face-up across my lap, leaning over you, shoving my mouth against you.

You are made helpless with my closing you in, trapping you with my hands, my arms, my body, and you reach up to me even as I smash my teeth into the softness of your lips, even as I cover your mouth and nose and stop you breathing.

 My need to have more of you is fed by having more of you. I always want more of you.

Under instruction

"Get on your knees."

"Stroke your cock (my cock)."

"Use my panties."

"Slower."

"Faster now."

"Put a nipple clamp on your left nipple."

"Stroke my cock gently."

"Put the other nipple clamp on your right nipple."

"More, softly, softly."

You are vocal, which I adore. My instructions punctuated by your audio-porn. Your moist-mouthed and laboured breathing makes me want to come. I am wet, of course. I bring my fingers to my pussy and touch myself while you do what I say. I feed you my arousal and you reflect it back to me magnified.

"Take the nipple clamps off, one at a time."

Your voice changes at the pain of it, whimpers, a sobbing. Our breathing and moans float desperate in the air. I can't tell which are yours and which are mine.

When I come, you make a strangled sound.

You are not allowed to come.

Enough

I am languid and relaxed, my hands are cold, I want to heat them on your skin, slide them against the warmest parts of you, then I want to casually reach out and slap your face, to have you kneeling here by me, so I can slap you and feel it resonate and then slap you some more and see if it makes me hungry, or if it's enough, just that.

Do you think it will be enough, baby?

SHY

Shy... well, shy is sweet—it's so delicate, it breaks my heart, just a little.

It makes me want to get right in his face, back him into a corner, and make that sweet shyness into excruciatingly uncomfortable, awkward, blushing, stammering and stuttering sink-into-the-ground self consciousness.

And when he tries desperately to break the tension, with that half-joking, half-hopeful, half-smile that shy people do sometimes, I want to feel his embarrassment when it doesn't work, and see in his face his fervent wishing that he was anywhere but right where he is right now.

Makes me want to grab and shove and push and wrap my fingers around his throat and kiss him so hard his head slams into the wall in that corner and his eyes open wide in shock.

Makes me want to transform it, that shy, into something else... into something worse, and then into something much much better.

I want to be inside his skin when he recognises that transition, and feel his heartbeat and his mouth and his breath and his thoughts and his cock when he realises that he's helpless, when he surrenders his awkward, excruciating self-consciousness to that surprising shock of pleasure, not sure if he should trust it, but wanting to, badly.

Shy... well, shy is sweet.

Needles

"How many, baby?"

You struggle to comprehend what I am asking. I see the shadow of confusion pass over your face as you try to focus, try to remember the last number, try to recall what we are up to...

"Ten?" Your voice raised in a question.

I shake my head, and I flick the ones I have thrust through the skin of your balls and cock one at a time, making you flinch as I count them slowly, there are eleven needles piercing you.

"There are already eleven there," I tell you.

You nod, barely cognisant.

"Eleven, yes Ma'am."

I reach for another one, the crackle of the plastic sounds loud in the room and you look up at me, blinking slowly, trying to pay attention ("Are you paying attention, boy?"). I take my time, stroking your cock gently, feeling the ridges of the needles through your skin, watching your face, blissed and trusting and beautiful.

I pinch the skin of your cock, bring the tip of the needle to it and penetrate you again, you gasp, your muscles tense and you let out a moan as your body accepts the violation. I continue, relentlessly sliding needles into you, and when I am finished, there are five needles in your balls, ten in your cock, one through each of your nipples.

Seventeen needles, baby.

I lean over to kiss you, gentle, soft against your lips, you are laid open, everything splayed. I hover over you, avoiding the needle points and you are melting under me, into my mouth. You reach for me when I pull back, the restraints preventing you lifting up far enough to stay with me.

"Seventeen needles, baby," I say out loud.

Your eyes meet mine. "Seventeen, Ma'am."

There are sixty-seven needles left in the box. We have time. You know that eventually we will use them all.

She watched him

She watched him, a sheen of sweat on his face, a picture of concentration. He glanced at her now and then, to check if she was watching, to see if she was paying attention to him. She was.

She sipped her wine, keeping her eyes on him, the cold liquid sliding down her throat, honey, melon, lemon. The apartment smelt of garlic, herbs and a sharp tang of vinegar.

She went to him and pressed herself against his back, wine glass in one hand, the other slipping around his body, under his t-shirt, touching him gently. She didn't need to see his face to feel his smile and his gentle pressing back against her, his movements slowing, but still, he chopped and mixed.

She brought her glass to his lips and watched his mouth open slightly as she tipped it and the liquid entered him. It made her stomach turn over with lust, that glimpse of his open mouth, the entering, his unquestioning compliance.

She closed her eyes and pressed against him, pushing her body into him, the lust in her throat now, rising to her mouth, her lips against his neck breathing him in, watching him cook for her.

She wanted to speak to him of love and tender hearts and awe and splendour and thanks and she wanted to gently, slowly, methodically, painfully eat him alive. She wondered if he felt it, these thoughts she sent to him as she pressed herself against him.

It didn't matter in the end. She felt it: that was enough.

Airport

I am tired and trying to work and thinking instead about shoving you into that corner at the airport, you, shy and uncertain, and I just want to get something from you, anything, right now, straight away, and I want to hear you, in my ear, in my mouth, breathe for me and gasp a little when I take your mouth and smash into your teeth and feel it reverberate and you have nowhere to back away to because you are already in that grubby corner and I push my hips forward and have an arm around your neck because your hair isn't long enough to grab and I pull your mouth to me and stand on my toes to make myself taller than you so I can put some force into the kiss that I am using to claim you, and I slip one hand under your shirt and touch your skin softly while I taste your mouth and your tongue and feel your lips moving under mine, and I concentrate on all that sparking, spiky, urgent energy, there, concentrated at our mouths, but I still reach for your nipples and let you feel me play my fingertips over them and I know you want me to, even though you have barely seen me for five minutes, you are already thinking about it and you want to say 'please, oh please...' but you daren't take your mouth from mine in case I pull away altogether, and I can feel you pushing your chest a little towards me, pleading with your body and when I tap at your nipple, you make a little yearning sound, and when I squeeze a little, pinch, twist, you make that beautiful sound into my mouth, that gasp-groan that goes straight to my cunt, and the promise of pain makes you thrust your hips towards me to get more contact on your cock even though I am already flush on you and I can feel you hard against me and I want to wrap my leg around you and pull you against me tighter and feel your cock pressed hard against my jeans-covered pussy and use it to rub myself on you.

BUTTON PUSHING

Before he leaves, there is more violent kissing, I shove him up against the fridge, banging his head against it, once, twice. He keeps his hands behind him: he doesn't touch me, he just stands helpless in the face of my attack as he moans into my mouth.

He reaches for me when I pull out of the kiss. He reaches for softness, straining to touch my lips with his, trying to keep contact with me, gentle, tender, as if he wants to counter the aggression, but I can feel him wishing, then, to draw me into brutality with his softness, to make me crazy with it.

He is learning already how to entice the violence up from the depths.

Good boy.

And then I come

You are restrained, spread-eagled and I sit on your chest, rocking my cunt against you to get off, my fingers on my clit, slapping your face telling you to beg to lick me, but you aren't doing it right, so rocking and slapping and telling you to beg me again, and you are so fucking frustrated and your neck and face ache from the slapping and you are trying over and over to get it right, getting more and more desperate and I keep telling you that I don't believe you really want it, and you are almost sobbing with trying to convince me that you do.

And then I come.

Table boy

I make you go and kneel in a corner and wait, where I can see you. You are not allowed to speak or move until I want you for something.

Finally I make you crawl to me.

"Here, boy."

I put my drink on your back, while I play my feet over your cock and your arse, and you know you had better not move or the drink will spill, and I ponder aloud whether I should fuck you, while I run my toes over you from your arse to your cock, applying some pressure, or, I ask myself, maybe I should smack your arse with your belt, over there, but either way you had better not spill my drink.

I stroke your cock with my foot and still you can't move, and of course my touch against you is too soft and I know you want to press against me to get more.

Occasionally I make you shift position a little ("face me, boy") so I can reach different parts of you, like your nipples, my drink again on your back, I torture your nipples and remind you that you had better not move, boy.

You make delicious sounds and desperately try to keep still and I am waiting for you to ask me to stop ("please please"), but you love it and hate it and you don't ask, you take it, and you do your very best, and I love that. You know I do, I love that.

The tallness of being

Man sees tall woman.

Man thinks, "God, she's frigging tall."

Man reasons, "She can't be that tall..."

Man glances down at woman's shoes.

Man registers heels. "Fuck are they ever high... and shiny... wow... is that normal?"

Man looks away.

Man looks at shoes again. "Jesus, those shoes are not NORMAL!"

Man looks at woman's face.

Woman looks at man.

Man blushes, caught.

NEXT.

WAITING

I hate to wait, I hate it, hate it, hate it. I have no patience... when I want something, I want it now now NOW...

And I am waiting...

I want to bring you into the room over and over, because once is not enough after all the waiting.

The first time, I will grab you around the neck and shove you up against the wall before you have a chance to get your bearings, squeeze your throat and watch your eyes widen in shock and I know your cock is hard, immediately, from the violence and the attack and the fear. I want to swear at you for making me wait, right in your face, spit at you.

"... fucking selfish little bitch... what are you?!"

And you will answer, small and scared. "... a fucking selfish little bitch, Ma'am, I'm sorry..."

I want to slap your face, hard, over and over and tell you to get your fucking clothes off, and you will struggle to do it because I am in your space and in the way, and slapping you, and you will try to give me access to your face, even while you are trying to undress, awkward and set upon...

The second time, I will pet you gently and draw

you into the room, stroking your short hair, your vulnerable neck, your beautiful face, and you will purr and lean into my touch, making beautiful soft sounds, and I will whisper to you.

"Welcome home baby."

And you will lock eyes with me and say, "I'm so happy to be home, Ma'am"

And I want to touch you all over, that skin that I have missed, alabaster soft and unmarked, just touch it, stroke it, feel it tremble under my fingertips, listen to your breathing change as my hands move all over you, soft and insistent and not enough for you, watch you blush when I slowly undress you, you standing self conscious and shy and happy...

The third time, I will put you on all fours, puppy, and lean down to you, saying, "Good boy, good boy", and pat your head, a gag immediately in your mouth, a collar around your neck, a leash connecting you to me, and I will undress you, stroking you down, cooing, "Who's a good boy then? I've missed you, boy, yes I have" and smacking at your arse as you awkwardly try to accommodate me while I am pulling off your clothes.

Cuffs joining your ankles make it hard for you to move, and I jerk the lead to make you follow me into the bathroom.

"Who needs a bath then, boy? Yes, you do, don't you?"

You look up at me (God, those wide puppy eyes),

and nod, trying not to drool through the gag. Another jerk on the lead and you climb into the bath...

The fourth time, I will kiss you. Kissing, boy, kissing, starting with tasting you as if I have never had you before, pulling your face down to me and stroking your lips with mine to feel their pillowy softness, nudging against your mouth a little, but holding off on having you open up to me, I want to make it slow and I want to make you wait as I have been waiting, to watch you reach for me the way you do, when you reach for softness and hope for violence.

The tip of my tongue just reaching out to touch your lips, just just just there and there and I feel yours seeking mine, but you can't have it yet, not yet, and more of that, kiss-chasey of our mouths, hot and breathy until I push harder against you and feel your sigh as you open up to me and let me in, and that that that makes me growl, makes me tense, I know you feel it and you make a sound because you know the violence is coming...

I hate to wait, hate it, hate it, hate it...

I am waiting...

A bedtime story

Once upon a time, there was a little boy, he was a sweet little boy, but when he looked around at the world, he was confused about how he fitted in. Sometimes, he would whisper to himself that it was okay, really. And sometimes, he would sneak off and find things to hurt himself with and hope that no-one would notice.

This little boy would find sweet little girls and kiss them. They would kiss him back, they liked him, those sweet little girls. And he would sometimes pretend that they were being mean to him when they were being gentle and lovely and kind.

Sometimes he showed them, shyly, how to be mean to him a little, but most times, he would wish it was so when it wasn't, and he would wish that he didn't think about it the way that he did.

The little boy started to find ways to make himself feel what he wanted to feel. He was bashful and embarrassed about it and pretended it wasn't really happening. He would look around his house for things to help him. He found belts and knives and cords, and when he was alone, he would try to use them on himself, to see what it felt like. But he never went out and bought any things that were specifically for that purpose, that would be wrong, that would mean he was strange and not quite right.

And the little boy imagined, while he hit himself, that there was a big girl, a mean girl standing over him making him do these things. He imagined that she would take that belt off him and hiss, "Let me SHOW you how it's done," and she would swing it at him while he knelt on the floor.

She would say horrible things to him, she would call him a filthy little bitch and a fucking slut and slap his face and make him crawl across the floor with his arse in the air and his face to the ground. She would be looking around the house for things to hurt him with, she would be eyeing off the umbrella, the wooden spoon, the knives. She would make him crawl all over the house to get these things for her and bring them to her in his mouth, one by one, while she smacked him every time he got close enough.

He imagined that she liked it, that she loved to see him confused and lost and small, that it made her wet, that it made her want more of him. He wanted her to hurt him more, he wanted her to force his face into her cunt, to stop him breathing, to cut him open, to fuck him so it would hurt, to open up his skin and his mouth and his chest and his stomach and shove her cock into all the holes.

He wanted her to slice pieces of him off his body, his nipples, holding them away from his body and sawing at them until she had them in her hand, then poking at the wounds with the knife, asking him, "Do you think I'm finished with you yet, bitch?'

And the boy would try to shake his head. "No, no, I don't think you are finished with me yet... I am still here... you haven't got it all yet."

When the boy finally passed out, the big girl lay down beside him. She poked her fingers and her cock and her tongue into the holes in him, touching him inside, gently at first, but it made her hungry and she wanted to wake him up so that she could fuck with him some more. She fucked into his arse with her cock, trying to bring him around by slapping his face so that he would fuck back against her, or fight her, or do something, but he wouldn't wake up.

She finally gave up and fucked at his lifeless body, different holes, trying to find the one that would give enough resistance to make her come. At the end, she fucked her cunt against his face, wet with blood and tears and saliva, until she came in his mouth. And she snuck out before he was found, a bloody beaten, stabbed, holey mess on the floor.

And she lived happily ever after.

Moments

Moments are swimming about in my head...

Your face open in anticipation when I move in to kiss you.

Your 'oh my god' after I stop you breathing and breathe for you.

Your expression when I fuck your arse face-to-face.

Your eyes when you are endorphined and struggling to focus.

Your delighted laugh when my coming makes me laugh with the sensory overload.

The sounds you make when I hurt you and then hurt you some more.

The way you concentrate when you are trying not to come.

Your movements under me when I cover you with my body and pin you down.

How you bring me what I need without my asking.

Your willing acceptance of my instructions.

The way you moan when you lick me.

Your furrowed brow when you are made shy.

How your eyes widen when you see a slap coming.

Your increasing confidence in touching me, reaching for me.

They way you flinch even though I know you want it, whatever 'it' is.

Your nervousness and excitement every time I come home.

Your gentle touches of my arm, my leg, my hand, when I am driving.

Your asking me to please put my collar on you over and again.

You naked and jaunty, then shy and embarrassed.

Your smile when I am being incredibly silly.

Your apology-sluttishness.

Your kisses on me, all over, everywhere.

Your body writhing when my teeth sink into your flesh.

Those exchanges that make us both laugh until we forget the point.

Your gentle nodding when you tell me, "I am happy..."

Sweat

It is quiet, there is no violence, no urgency. I am working on him, moving him into position, manipulating limbs, pulling and pushing at him. He starts to sweat, the moisture collecting between his shoulder blades, I continue to gently put pressure on him, he moves very little unless I tell him to, a tiny shift, a rolling of muscles.

I check his face, his eyes clear, his breathing even, his forehead beaded with sweat, his body showing no other signs of stress, just the sweat.

"How are you doing, baby?"

He meets my gaze and nods. "Good, Ma'am."

The wetness runs down his back in rivulets, I touch the moisture with my fingertips, turn my attention back to what I am doing, I am not done with him yet.

WAKE UP

She opens the door, he is snuggled under the blankets, his head hidden. She takes a moment before she steps into the room and climbs onto the bed. She uncovers his face.

He half smiles as he feels the bed take her weight, snuffling into the pillow, warm and cozy, awaiting her good morning kisses, anticipating her touch, he loves it when she wakes him.

She grabs his cuffed wrists quickly and joins them together with a clip. He starts to move, instinct, protest. She shoves his hands above his head and straddles him. He is trying to wake up in a hurry now. She slides up his body, and shoves her cunt against his mouth, she feels more than hears him.

"Oh!"

His mouth moves against her, his tongue, he starts to make a sound as he laps at her. She leans forward against the wall, her knees putting her body weight on his arms, she rocks against his mouth.

She presses her forehead against the wall, concentrating on his tongue, fucking his mouth, slow at first and long strokes, then getting faster, shorter, more violent. His body starts to writhe in time with her movements, he fucks the air as his senses are filled with her cunt, he struggles to breathe, licking at her as she shoves herself against him.

Suddenly she pulls away, his mouth follows her, cranes his neck to reach for her. She shuffles her wet pussy down his body, out of reach, he makes a small sound of loss, breathing heavily, she rocks her cunt against his heaving chest, he looks up at her, moaning softly, his tongue on his lips, his eyes clouded with want.

She slaps him, once, he grunts, returning his gaze to her. She slaps him again, three times, then again, and again, again, again. She gets off him and leaves the room without a word, slamming the door behind her.

Sleep kisses

I shuffle back until I am flush against him, his chest, stomach, cock pressed against me, warm, comforting, I pull his arm around me, the cuff cold between my breasts. I rock him gently, back and forth, back and forth, so tired, but I miss him when his mouth is not accessible to me, when I can't see his face, when I can't pet his puppy head. I have to turn around to face him, to reach for his mouth again, one last kiss before I fall asleep, legs entwined, his body pulled against mine, just one more, one more...

I wake in his arms, his lips soft against mine, gentle, tender, heartbreaking kisses, my mouth moves under his, I murmur, "Oh, I fell asleep kissing you baby..."

"No," he whispers. "I was kissing you awake..."

Oh god, just... oh... god...

Trust and fear

He gazes up at me, trust, I tell him what I want, he looks scared, he starts to shake. His face contorts as he tries to comply, he is embarrassed, mortified, insecure, he looks like he might cry, he apologises.

His open vulnerability is stunning, beautiful, I feel myself melt, it starts at my cunt and spreads from there, I stroke him, his shaking doesn't abate, his expression tortured, it makes me want to absorb him into me, to cover him with my body, to hold him down so he can't disappear, to wrap myself around him and make him safe from me.

I wrap my arms around his head, a cocoon, dark, our breath mixing in the warm space, his body trembling under mine, kissing, stroking, whispering, "It's okay baby, it's okay..."

It's okay baby, it's okay.

Collar

You come to me and kneel. You hand me the collar, the collar that I have given you, my collar, leather and steel, the engraving claiming you as my property.

"Please Ma'am, will you put your collar on me?"

It makes me smile every time you ask me. Every single time. It makes me melt, it brings you close, sometimes I reach to kiss you, and always, I say "Yes."

I put the collar around your neck as you kneel before me. You lean down, bring your face into my lap and you rest there, your skin warm against me, waiting for me to affix the clasp, to close the padlock. You feel it slip into place, hear it click shut and you raise your face to me, all soft and open affection, your eyes a question mark, sweetly hoping for a kiss.

And tonight, for the first time, you have to put it on yourself, my collar, and I am happy that you have it and I love that you will wear it, and I am heartbroken that I am not there to put it around your neck.

You ask me, "Please Ma'am, may I put your collar on?" and it makes me melt and it makes me so intensely sad, and I feel something crack a little.

"Yes, baby, yes, put it on…"

PREY

It is in the way you surrender, a quiet, unspoken, gentle offering of yourself, inevitable, unquestioning.

It is in the way you bow your head and wait, even without experience, you know, like you have seen inside my head, you understand exactly how to elicit that aggressive response from me, to raise that hunger that you love.

It is in the way you look sideways at me, find the courage to be cocky, checking, checking that you haven't gone too far ('too far? am I still okay? is this okay?').

It is in the way you care for me, call me sweetheart, baby love, want to wrap me up, look after me.

It is in the way you tilt your head to lean against me; weighty, solid, offering me your puppy head to pet.

It is in the way you bump into me when we walk, reach for my hand, looking for ways to touch me, seek contact, anything, crave it.

It is in the way you let the fear show, on your face, in your body, in your voice, you know I love that.

It is in the way your anticipation moves and breathes, like it lives outside of you, exists just to lead me into the chase.

You are prey. It is not passive, it is not a stillness... it is movement and dance and invitation and offering, a distress signal sent straight to my heart.

You are prey... you are good at it.

Petting

We are watching television. He sits on the ground beside the couch, at my feet, a cushion I bought for ten cents at the school fete under his arse to keep him off the cold tiles. The 'butt cushion' I have dubbed it because it makes me laugh.

I can feel his energy as he sits there quietly. It emanates from him in waves, invisible threads drawing me in. I feel the pull in my fingertips, in the pit of my stomach and I know if I reach out and touch him, he will lean into it and silently vibrate with pleasure, not asking for more, but wanting more.

I shift slightly and he turns his head a little, acknowledging my movement, ready for me to say something, do something, want something. I wait until he settles again, like a restless pet finding a comfortable position. It makes me smile.

I reach out and touch his hair, crew cut and baby-soft, my puppy head, I stroke it, enjoying the feel of his fur, the way it grows in different directions, the soft resistance as I pet him. He tries not to move, to accept my attention without comment, but he adjusts his body bit by bit, slightly, almost imperceptibly as the stroking gets his attention.

I make a rhythm of the petting, a metronome of movement and I hear his breathing deepen as he sinks into it. I know he is not watching television any more, he is just concentrating on my touch, on the repetitive stroking stroking stroking. I can almost hear him whispering, "Please please please", but he is silent, the slightest leaning into my fingertips.

I smile.

As always

I am thinking, as always, about kissing you, about your mouth, how it shapes that 'oh' of anticipation when I bring my lips close to you, how you wait wait wait and try so hard not to reach for me, they are almost unbearable, those moments of denial.

I am torn, as always, by what I want, by wanting it all at once, by wanting to take it and have it and leave nothing behind.

I want the gentle, tender, moist, licking kisses, those that make you moan softly, those that make you melt away, those that let me taste you slowly, where I get to lap at you, to share the air between us, to suck gently at you, to inhale your desire slowly from your mouth, delicate and ethereal.

I want, also, like a greedy child, to devour you now, now, now... to shove you back into the wall, to smash your head against it and hear the crack, to open my mouth, uncover my carnivorous fangs and have at you, to close my teeth against your soft lips, to feel your body squirming even as you try to give me what I need, to rip them off you, those lips, leaving your mouth agape, a startled rictus, then take also your tongue, pulling it into my mouth with all the force I can muster, feeling my teeth ache to rip it from you by the root, your cock hard with pain and fear.

I am thinking, as always, about kissing.

"You hit me…"

I am straddling his chest, he is writhing underneath me, his body in constant motion, seeking something more, reaching, searching, his movements limited by my weight on him, by the cuffs joining his hands above his head. He is not fighting me, but he can't keep still, he makes small sounds into the room.

I reach down to position his head and I slap him, hard, across his cheek, the sting of it tight and harsh.

All of his movement stops in the aftermath of the strike. Suddenly he is still, like a switch has been flicked. He is shocked. The stillness surprises me. His wide eyes meet mine…

"You hit me…"

He states it like a fact, which it is, but he is shocked by it, as if I have never slapped him before, as if he is a nice vanilla boy on whom I have inflicted some outrage, as if he can't quite believe I did it.

I want to laugh, I am confused by his reaction, by his paralysis, his surprise.

"Yes, baby, I hit you." I confirm it for him.

He nods slowly, his eyes cloudy, unfocussed. I wonder where he has disappeared to, but he is truly gone, his body slack, his mouth half open, he lies under me as if he cannot move, as if he is bound to the bed, as if I have rendered him helpless with the slap.

I no longer want to laugh, I am gazing down at him in wonder at the way he slips under like that, just like that... I lean down to kiss him, he barely responds, I don't stop until he is back with me, his body slowly rising from the depths of the place he has been, until he kisses me back.

There you are... there you are, beautiful... hello baby, welcome back...

CUTTING TO THE CORE

He feels it more deeply now, everything cuts to the core of him. She hurts and scares and thrills him. He is so beautiful, still shy and afraid, but he discards the pretence, that thin veneer. He reaches to open himself even further to her, the slide into oblivion so close, always right there. He knows she loves his vulnerability—he steps bravely into the void and shows it to her, offered up with trust.

He knows now that she will not stop when he is hurt beyond hurt, when he bleeds, or when he hovers on that edge, so he lets her see it, raw and real, that wildness in his eyes, the screaming pain, the helpless cries.

He is coming into his own... he is coming home to her and it makes her stupidly proud, makes her mouth and fingertips tingle with want, makes her feel like she can't contain it inside her skin, makes her want to wrap him up into some small thing, to carry him with her, to absorb him into her pores and suck him into her mouth.

She examines it, this feeling, and finds, to her surprise, that it is her heart breaking. Over and over, he breaks her heart.

Marking territory

I push him down to his knees and pull his mouth against me. He shoves his face into my cunt and licks at me, eager, desperate. I let him thrust his tongue into me, hold him hard against me, shove my hips towards him, his movements insistent and rhythmic, I close my eyes and relax into him. I push-pull at his head, moving it away from me, turning it, he fights me, kisses whatever part of my body he can reach, his lips and tongue caressing my skin, I feel him angling to get back to my cunt.

"I'm going to mark you," I tell him softly.

He nods against my leg. "Yes, please Ma'am."

He leans into me, turns his head to kiss my thigh, rubs his cheek against my skin.

I rock myself against him, concentrating. He waits, but can't keep still, turning his face into my thigh, my cunt, licking at me until I push his head away, his tongue and attention distracting me. Finally, a tentative stream trickles warmly over his cheek, his shoulder, he makes a sound and turns his face into me.

I feel him licking at me, trying to catch the liquid in his mouth, I pull him closer against me. The stream is stronger now, and I feel him swallowing, his mouth and throat working, desperately trying to make a seal against my cunt, sucking at me.

He drinks from me, I am inside and all over him, marking him as mine. I have to concentrate so as to not be distracted by his mouth on me, trying to get inside me. When the flow slows and finally stops, he still licks at me, seeking to stay connected, I stroke his head gently, holding him against me.

When I step back I feel his disappointment, his loss. I lean down and look into his doe eyes, he meets my gaze, his breathing audibly strained in the silence, a slight moaning in the back of his throat communicating with me, he is so close so close.

I kiss him gently, I am thinking 'mine', but I say nothing.

Caning

They go to a caning workshop, sit on the comfortable couch, touching gently, watching the woman in leather deftly wield the instruments, listening intently to her explanations as she demonstrates her craft.

She strokes his puppy head, he shifts closer to touch more of her, she leans into him now and then to whisper about what they are seeing.

She had never been so interested in canes, she is not a sadist (she sees him smile at that, a soft, amused "yes Ma'am" wanting to trip off his tongue, she shushes him and continues...), she is not a sadist, so has never been so much interested in the hardness, the unforgiving nature of canes. This one, though, this boy, has some depth of masochism that she hasn't seen before, she doesn't attract the masochistic boys, but she has one now and she wants to see where she can take him. She watches, and learns.

Later, she has him tied over a bench, bent over, naked and exposed. She touches him gently, he quivers, he is afraid. She leans down to kiss him and she can feel him drawing comfort from her, sucking her courage into him. She strokes his body down, like he is a wild thing that needs calming, then steps back, hefting the cane, getting used to its weight, its length.

She starts softly on his arse, judging the distance, the angle of the strikes, watching the slight marks appear. He lifts up to her, offering himself, it makes her smile. A flick is enough to see a reaction, she holds the cane lightly, gaining confidence, taking her time: They have all the time in the world.

The rhythm comes easily, she finds her stride. Steady at first, she changes it up, faster, then slow, a few hard strikes in a row, the sound cuts into the room, harsh and sharp. She checks the marks, she whispers to him, she kisses him, he starts to lose focus.

"Are you paying attention, boy?" she asks.

"Yes Ma'am," he murmurs. "While I can still kiss you I am okay Ma'am."

She laughs and continues.

Some time later, his arse is a mess, his thighs, his calves show the marks of her enthusiasm also. He squirms away from her strikes, his knees bending sideways as he tries to escape the next hit, he is silent, his face is resting against the bench, a puddle of spit is flowing away from his mouth. When she leans down to him, his unseeing eyes barely register her presence, when she closes in for a kiss he no longer reaches for her. He is high on the pain, he has drifted away from her, he is floating, he has had enough.

She looks at his arse, it is darkly purple-bruised, pulpy, like ripe fruit, she touches it with her fingertips and he moans, she can feel the blood right under the skin, a few more strikes and she would break through to blood-splatter.

She unties him, he gazes at her, surrender and hope, he can barely move. She helps him up and leads him to the bed.

"I'm not done with you yet, boy," she whispers.

He nods. "Yes Ma'am, I'm glad."

Violence

I don't want 'play': the pretty, the tools, the toys, the games, the amusement, the cute, the acts, the implements, the controlled, the measured give and take, the things.

I want violence: force and shoving and slapping and tearing at flesh and smashing you to the ground and not giving a fuck about you. I want fear and helplessness and tears and surrender and panic and animal lust. I want growling and screaming and grunting and gasping for breath. I want that fucking violence, that desperation, that grabbing selfish need, messy and passionate and out of control.

I miss it.

Where the fuck are you?

Say...

We are on Skype having a chat when his phone rings. He is expecting a call, excuses himself, picks it up. I stay online and listen to his end of the conversation, waiting for him to finish. I get a little bored and send him an instant message.

"Say 'horrendous'."

He messages back, "Yes Ma'am..."

There is a smile in his voice as he continues his conversation. I can hear him stifling the grin as he thinks about it.

A minute or so later, I hear him say in exaggerated disbelief, "That's horrendous!!"

I giggle like a six year old girl, he is trying not to snigger. I try another one.

"Say 'reprehensible'," I message him.

"Yes Ma'am."

I can hardly stop laughing as I listen, his attention is distracted now, he is trying to work it into the conversation.

A short while later he says, "Would she really do something so reprehensible?!"

I am laughing so hard I have tears in my eyes. He sounds like a demented child showing off words he has just learnt in kindergarten. I am absolutely delighted with this game.

I think of another one...

Kissing noises

You make kissing noises at me, from the side there, not really looking at me. I smile and watch your mouth, your lips pressing together, pursing, then opening slightly, you are trying not to smile back at me, your face deliberately and cutely serious, the gentle sucking noise soft and moist and enticing.

"Are you making kissing noises at me?"

You smirk. "Of course, Ma'am!"

I laugh and grab the back of your head and pull your mouth to me, you open immediately, and I feel you become soft and pliant, while your body gets hard and desperate, like a switch has been flicked. You moan softly into my mouth, straight into me, I swallow it and reach for more.

I lean back a little and you follow me with your mouth, reluctant to lose contact, seeking, chasing, leading with your lips, your tongue reaching for me, we are locked at the mouth. I pull back further until you can't reach me anymore without stepping forward, you reluctantly let me go.

We look at each other, you are waiting, chest heaving, mouth slightly open, you lick your lips, your eyes on mine, I watch your tongue snake out and lap at your lips, your unconscious tease making me tense, I feel the corner of my mouth curl up at you, I see the question in your eyes.

I wrap my hand around your throat, you close your eyes briefly as I squeeze a little. I lean forward to get closer to your mouth and you throw yourself suddenly against the hand around your throat to get at me. I hold firm, trying not to step back under the force of your assault, you choke yourself against me, your mouth open, a guttural sound coming out of your restricted windpipe, I lean my mouth closer to yours, but still not within reach, and you redouble your efforts, gagging yourself and struggling to breathe, my fingers tight around your neck.

The sounds coming from your constricted throat are loud in the room, like a wounded animal caught in a trap, desperately trying to breathe, but still you shove yourself against me. I have to use all of my strength, concentrated on my hand around your throat, to hold you back. You don't ease up, your face reddening, the veins in your neck throbbing and pumping, you strangle yourself to get at me.

I ease the pressure against your neck and your mouth is suddenly and desperately on mine again. I am rabid now and with teeth clashing and your soft lips between, I attack your mouth, sucking up the breath you have worked so hard to get, clashing against you, denying you, still, the air you need and you struggle between the gasping and this thing which is no longer really kissing except in the remotest sense with mouths and tongues and teeth and lips.

When I pull away again, I can see the determination in your eyes and feel you press against my fingers, ready to be strangled, wanting it, in the split second before I shake my head slightly, tighten my grip around your throat and shove you back, hard. You are taken by surprise, off balance, and one, two steps backwards, you fall back against the bed, sprawled there, you look up at me, sucking in air in huge heaving gasps. I take a step towards you.

Arse show

I watch you sleep. I do that sometimes, it is sweet. You snuffle and shift and occasionally you mutter to yourself.

Tonight, you have half thrown the covers off, you are curled up facing away from me, and your pretty arse is exposed. Your pose is childlike, unintentionally provocative, and completely slutty, like you planned it this way, like you are smiling secretly to yourself at your own cleverness.

I sent you to bed with the crotchless stockings still on. I realise they are gone, somehow. I know you wouldn't have taken them off (did you take them off?! did you dare?!). I find out later that they have bunched up around your ankles, restraining you, and I wish that I had known that at the time when I was watching you, that you were tied up by the nylons and restrained that way.

Your skin is alabaster white and untouched, virginal and oh, you shift again, making a soft smacking, sucking sound with your mouth, pushing your arse towards me, an invitation.

I can't see your face, I wonder if you are awake and teasing me.

I whisper to you, "It's okay baby, sssshhhh... it's okay," to see if you will talk to me, but you are silent then and settle back into slumber.

I am excited by this wanton innocence, this accidental peep show, you shift now and then, never showing me more, your legs pressed primly together, your arse smooth, your cheeks round and full and the crack of it drawing a line down to lead my eyes to the tops of your thighs. I wet my lips with my tongue and silently watch you like some creepy stalker.

I don't even feel predatory really, I feel sly and dirty, furtive, filthy, like I want to sully your innocence. Like I want to masturbate and come on your pristine skin. Like I want to stick you with a needle full of drugs to immobilise you and then fuck your lifeless body. Like I want to touch you and grab and probe at your pliant stillness without your knowledge. Like I want to cover your slack mouth with my cunt and stop you breathing until your unconscious body finds some panic button and bucks and shakes before it gives up.

I am ridiculously disappointed when you roll over, cover yourself, hide from me. I reluctantly let the dirty peeping tom in me subside and tuck her away for later.

Don't care

He looks over at me.

"... and anyway, I don't care what you think," he says.

There is a pause as I look back at him.

We both erupt into giggles at the same time.

"I was trying so hard not to laugh...!!" he says, still giggling like a small child.

I am almost on the floor with laughter.

"Yeah, I know..."

My cocks

I like having a cock. That swaggering heaviness, that obvious, out-there fuck toy, the potential to hurt or to give pleasure right there in it, sticking out like some wanton slut soliciting for business.

It is blatantly sexy, it's another way to fuck with him and fuck him, another way to make him get that look, that lost distance that tells me he is gone, that yearning hopeless gaze, that grunting whimpering desperation that lets me know, even when he's mindless in it, that he's mine.

Many of the things I want to force onto a boy, the things in my head that are madly and insanely hot, involve both terrible violence and getting off from forcing and shoving and hurting and not caring about anything except using him to make me come. Cocks give men the ability to take pleasure, to 'force' someone to get them off, and that's pretty fucking hot.

My mind takes me there, into those dark places, it is a mire of hopeless, cold, unforgiving sexual violence coupled with a detached disinterest in the target of those urges.

When I am in it, I just want to use him and take take take.

If I had a real flesh and blood cock, I would be forcing it into my boy non-stop: not just his mouth and his arse, I'd be shoving it between his legs, into armpits, behind knees, between arse cheeks, into hands, but mostly, mostly I would be thrusting it into his beautiful mouth stretched wide, making him drool and struggle to breathe, shoving it into his throat until he gags around it, fucking that wet softness hard, slamming his head into a wall, the floor, it doesn't matter what, and I would come every time, from forcing my pleasure onto him whenever and however I want.

He wears…

1. My collar.
   Leather and steel, engraved with my claim on him as my property. There is a ritual in putting it on and taking it off. He kneels and asks me if he may put it on. I say yes (of course, I say yes!). It is locked around his neck with a small padlock. He must ask, also, if he needs to take it off. It is beautiful on him.
2. A leather bracelet with my initial on it.
   A sort of charm. He wears it always.
3. A red yarn around his wrist.
   It is historical, since forever it seems, he has worn something at my behest, before I owned him, before we knew what this was, he has worn a yarn for me.
4. A red yarn around my cock.
   He has worn it as long as the one around his wrist. It is my cock, it just happens to be attached to him, attached to that body, which is mine also… He keeps it safe for me.
5. Whatever underwear I tell him to wear each day.
   Mostly boxers, black or grey, and sometimes panties, mine, lacy and sweet.

6. Whatever I tell him to wear to bed.
   Usually my collar and nothing else. I like him naked, but sometimes, sometimes, when he needs to feel secure and warm and swathed, I have him wear boxers and t-shirt.
7. Writing on his body.
   It is almost a fetish for me and it is rare now that I let him go out into the world without my marks on him. Maybe kisses on his hip, my initials over his heart (mine), my name on my cock, messages reminding him of his place ('owned property', 'beautiful boy').

I don't want him to forget for one second that he is mine.

Buckling

I am crouching in front of him, his hard cock (my cock) in front of my face, but I am not interested in the cock right now.

I am nipping at him, biting, which is the thing that has driven him closest to safe wording with me. I nuzzle at his skin, lips and softness, tongue lapping at him, he pushes his flesh towards me, flinching when I close my teeth on it. I push my face between his legs, he widens his stance. I suck the soft flesh of his inner thighs into my mouth and suddenly snap my teeth shut on pieces of him, he is making sounds above me, but I barely hear him, his cock bobs as he moves, gently tapping against me, insistently wanting attention. I ignore it and travel the sensitive places...

Bitebitebitebitenuzzlelicksipsucknibblebite bite BITE BITE.

The biting is punctuated with his groans, his exclamations of pain, his gasps of pleasure. When it gets too much, he tries to pull away from me, which makes me drive my fangs through his skin to pull him back to me, to keep him in his place.

I can't see his face, but I know his expression; eyes squeezed shut, mouth open in a grimace, sucking back his saliva, trying not to move. He wants to rock himself, to move, he wants more, he wants it to stop.

I fist his cock and hold it up against his stomach, out of my way. He moans softly at the contact, but I am not interested in the cock right now. I lap at his balls, I know it scares him: I have been biting. I nestle into and against him softly, my cheek against his thigh. I nibble gently at the tender skin, mouthing him, sucking and licking, he is scared, I can feel it, I snap at him and all his muscles tense, my teeth half closed, he waits, a pained sound coming from above me. I let his ball slip out of my mouth and feel him relax a little with relief. In the momentary lapse, I lunge forward, suck his right ball partially into my mouth and I bite down HARD.

He cries out, buckles, doubling over, falling onto the bed, a strangled noise escapes his lips, turning into a sobbing sound, he curls up into a foetal position, gasping for air. I crawl up beside him and cover him with my body

"Oh baby..." I coo at him. "Oh poor baby..."

Blur

He is tied down, face up when I come back to him and all is a blur, a strobe light of glimpses and moments, time is disjointed and I look at the disarray around me and know that I caused it.

Waxing, nipple clamps, biting, cock slapping, tiny holes from the wartenberg wheel, smacking all over, biting biting, shocking, ball stretching, a chain in his mouth, metallic kissing, desperate breathing, riding his mouth, struggling, teeth so many teeth, fear, cropping his cock, nipples, inner thighs, my tongue nearly on his cock, gasping, pulling at skin, more kissing, my nipple in his mouth, groaning, feet on his face, ripping, toes in his mouth, trembling, tasting skin, blood, smacking, rubbing, thrusting, twisting, squeezing, moaning.

I smash into him harder and harder, brutally, like he is a thing in my way, like I have to get past him, through him, over and over.

And then I come.

The corner

We are sitting close, touching, stroking, heading home after an evening out with friends.

"I can't wait until we get home and do some kissing..."

I shake my head. "No kissing..." I whisper.

He smiles at me, amused and puzzled.

"No kissing?!"

I smile back and lean into him. "No."

"Cuddling?"

"No, when we get home, you are going to stand naked in the corner..."

He laughs, I look at him, he cocks his head at me.

"No kissing?"

"No... naked in the corner."

"No lying down?"

"No."

"Blanket?"

"No."

"Boxers?"

"No... naked in the corner..."

"Snacks?"

"No."

"TV?"

"No."
"Kissing?"
"No."
He snuggles closer into me,
"Okay Ma'am."

Impact

Flesh on flesh, I am shoving at him, keeping my body off his cock (my cock), no contact there, but otherwise I am all over him with limbs everywhere, skin slipping against him, my mouth open and demanding, feeding off him with the violence of need. He is splayed open on the bed and I am pushing and smashing against him. He is desperate to do what I want, aroused and hungry and confused.

I want his arse, my fingers, my knuckles pushing against the sensitive skin, thrusting against him, grabbing roughly at his balls. He tries to open himself to me, I look around quickly, I have no lube within reach, my strap-on over there. I am frustrated, there is no way I am going to leave him, not for a second, not when I am like this.

I shove his knees over to one side, he is awkward there, his mouth reaching up for me, his lower body almost foetal, twisted and awkward. I am looming and I thrust against his arse with my hips, trying to fuck him with my cunt, widening my stance to go harder at him, trying to get inside him. He makes a desperate moaning sound as I fuck at him, like I am fucking him, the movement forces his head to smack up against the wall. The solid thud of the impact speaks to me like love and I fuck him harder, pulling him against me and forcing his head ever more brutally into the wall, a deep vicious satisfaction in the thump I feel through his body at each impact. He makes a whimpering sound, a grunting each time he hits the wall, his face shocked at the impact over and again, though he knows it's coming, of course he knows.

I glance, again, over at the strap-on, over there. I am reluctant, so reluctant to let go of him... I just want to get lost in this, but I want more, always more. I am so fucking loathe to lose contact, I slow down my movement against him. I kiss him, hard aggressive, biting at him, he fights to get more of me, then I push myself off him and cross the room.

Shoe shopping

We wander into the sex shop in the gay part of town. It is a rather conventional shop, by most standards, but oh, they have shoes. Stripper shoes a mile high, with clear heels and diamantes, platforms in white, red and black, ribbons and shiny leather.

I search through sizes while he idly browses beside me. I point some out to him.

"Look, look at these, these are fabulous!!"

He smiles and nods approval. "Yes Ma'am."

I find a size 13 and beckon him over. It takes him a second to realise that they are for him.

"Try them on." My voice is loud in the small space.

He looks around, there is a man behind the counter, another browsing, a woman also. He nods and takes them from me, placing them on the floor.

He slips his shoes and socks off and tries, awkwardly, to squeeze his foot into the right shoe. It is so high, it throws him off balance. He grabs onto the shelf to steady himself. I crouch in front of him to do it up, and help him get the left shoe on, I roll his jeans up so that I can see them. He towers above me when I stand, probably 6'6 in these crazy heels. He totters, like a stilt-walker, trying to balance.

I laugh at him. He blushes and smiles back, he is concentrating on not falling over.

I hold out my hands to him.

"Come on."

He takes my hands and I encourage him to walk to me. He teeters precariously, barely able to take a few steps. The man who was browsing is watching, an amused smile on his face.

I catch his eye over my boy's shoulder.

"Don't they look sweet on him?" I ask.

He grins at me. "Oh yes, yes they do... he needs some practice, though, love."

"He does, doesn't he?"

We are complicit in embarrassing him, both amused.

The other man comes out from behind the counter, to have a look.

"What do you think? They're pretty on him, aren't they?" I ask him.

He looks my boy up and down, a quick assessment. He nods.

"They ARE pretty."

He smiles and leans against the shelf, happy to stand there and watch.

I keep an eye on my boy's face to see how he is taking it. They are behind him and he pretends he hasn't heard, looking down at his feet, his brow furrowed as he tries to take a few more steps, holding my hands for support. His concentration is incredibly sweet, and finally he looks up at me, a sideways half smile on his face. He is embarrassed, and proud, and I can see he is a little glazed, like he gets when he is caught up in doing things for me.

"Hard isn't it?" I ask him.

I see the momentary flash of confusion when he thinks I might be referring to his cock (a thought that nearly makes me laugh out loud).

He nods. "Oh god, yes Ma'am."

I make him take a few more awkward halting steps, like a baby giraffe, then lead him slowly down the aisle and back. One of the men offers advice to me on how to improve his walk, make it more confident, sexy... it involves him swaying his hips, we discuss him as if he isn't there. Finally, I relent and indicate that we are done. The men drift away when they see that the show is over.

I help him take the shoes off and he steps down from them like a stepladder. I stand close to him when he is back on solid ground.

He has dropped into his space and I love that, adore it, it is like a beacon for me. I lean up to him and rub my cheek against his, he presses against me for a moment and I hold him there, a hand around his neck.

"That was difficult for you, wasn't it?" I whisper into his ear.

He nods against me. "Yes, Ma'am."

I hold him close and he softens into me.

"Good boy," I say.
I feel him smile against my cheek.
"Thank you Ma'am."

Pieces of skin and bone

I want very much to tell you stories and lovely things and send you snipped locks of hair and have you give me pieces of skin and bone and fix it all with you here so that we can fight and make up like we are a regular Joe and Mary (that's you, by the way, Mary), and make you stand naked in the corner and write penance with your tongue on the wall and have you kneeling and pretty and spanked and nipped and petted and slapped and kisses baby.

Good puppy

I put a collar and leash on him, lead him on all fours into the bathroom. I have him climb into the tub for his bath, the leash tied to the taps. I scrub him all over, teasing him, roughly washing his hair and face. He shakes his head like a puppy, water flinging off his face. It makes me laugh. Then I dry him, utilitarian, forcefully rubbing at his skin, talking to him about what a good boy he was for the washing.

Naked, collared and cuffed, I wrap his hands in ripped cloth and duct tape: paws. I feed him breakfast: bananas, cereal, yoghurt. His face sweetly dips down to the bowl on the floor, his arse in the air. I scrape the plate with my fingers and let him lick and suck them clean. I put a bowl of water on the floor. I talk to him, idly, like you talk to your dog.

Later, we watch a movie. Puppy is allowed on the bed, snuggled beside me.

I make some comment about what's on screen, he answers me, laughing. It takes us both a few seconds to realise that he has spoken. I raise my eyebrows at him. Comically, his wrapped paws fly to cover his mouth, his eyes widen, a look of shock and horror frozen on his face.

"Can puppies talk?!" I demand.

He shakes his head, his hands still over his mouth, his pretty eyes staring at me in a parody of fear, like a cartoon character. I want to laugh.

I grab him by the collar, pull him over my lap and smack him as hard as I can on his arse. A stereotypical 'bad dog' spanking, a word with every strike.

"Puppies. Can't. Talk. Can. They?!! No. They. Can't. And. You. Know. That…"

I hit him until I have run out of words and my hand gets sore and his arse is pink. When I am done, he whimpers and snuggles in beside me again.

I restart the movie.

Please hurt me

He was shocked and bewildered and lost. Our play had hit something at the core of him and he looked stricken, chest heaving, face screwed up, on the edge of tears. I cradled him, rocking him gently, kissing, crooning to him.

"It's okay baby, it's okay." I stroked his face.

He looked up at me, a little boy, scared and bewildered.

"Please hurt me..." he asked in a small voice. "Please...?"

I understood at once that he was asking me to bring him back from it, to ground him, to give him something solid to hang onto. I wanted to keep him here with me, this almost broken boy, and gently coax him out of it, but he needed something else.

"Yes, baby, yes... it's okay..."

I spread him out, his anticipation palpable and a little desperate, his need trembling between us.

And then I started to hurt him.

Can I...?

He is washing her, kneeling before her, warm water cascading over their bodies, his hands gliding over her soapy skin. She reaches down for a kiss, he opens his mouth to her and she tastes him in the wetness, it makes her sigh with pleasure.

He whispers something to her that she doesn't quite hear... He is embarrassed, shy, unable to look at her. She makes him repeat it.

"Can I... put my tongue inside you, Ma'am?" whisper-soft and hesitant.

It is an odd request and so specifically worded. She looks askance at him, puzzled. He blushes, mortified at himself, but doesn't elaborate.

She shakes her head. "You can do exactly what I say you can do... no more..."

He shakes his head also, disappointment and rejection written all over his face.

She touches his cheek and turns so that he can wash her back.

Blindfold

She ties him to the bed, face up, cuffs on wrists and ankles, spread-eagled, open for her, helpless, hard, exposed.

Then, a blindfold.

She hasn't used one for a while, the darkness scares him, she can see it in the way he shies away from her hands, trying to sink into the bed, the way he licks his lips (she watches his tongue slip out of his mouth and lap nervously at the sides of his mouth, it makes her stomach lurch, her mouth opens slightly, almost involuntarily, she hears her own breathing, her eyes on his lips, she shakes the thought loose, kissing would be too familiar to him, too comforting, it is not what she wants).

She moves around the room, getting things ready. She takes her time, keeping an eye on him. She can feel the fear growing in him, she can taste it, it makes her smile.

Sounds of zippers, rummaging in bags, crackling plastic, soft footsteps, her swish as she passes the bed, the slight movement as she places things beside him.

His breath is coming quicker now, shallow, he is trying to be silent so that he can hear her, place her in the room. She knows that his heart is racing by now, that he wants to be touched so badly that his skin aches, that he desperately wants it to start, whatever 'it' is, that he can't bear this empty space between now and then.

He starts to squirm.

I know...

We go to a kinky film festival—short films, an arts centre out in the middle of nowhere. The ticket collector is a big man decked out head-to-toe in a pink frilly little girl's outfit—from pink sequined shoes to pink ruffled bonnet. He is carrying a giant multi coloured lollipop. I love that. To my disappointment, he is the only one who has 'dressed' for the occasion.

I am wearing killer heels, jeans, a sparkly black top. My lips are, just for the event, a dark glossy red, an aggressive bold colour, a colour I never wear.

We watch the short films, a couple are interesting, some funny, most not even mildly erotic. We hold hands in the dark and I cross my leg over his, he pulls me against him. We are cocooned there together, sweetly wrapped up, we whisper in between each film, we don't care about the movies so much.

Afterwards, they have interviews with some of the directors and actors in the films. We sit through quite a few, and ironically, just as I let my boy know that we are leaving, and we get up and move towards the door, the speaker starts talking about short attention spans... I pinch my boy's arm and we stifle giggles like children.

We get out of the cinema, laughing. There are some people milling about. He helps me into my coat and I hear one of the men waiting in the foyer say something to my boy.

He replies, matter of fact, "I know…"

When we get outside, I ask what he wanted, the stranger.

My boy shrugs. "He just wanted to tell me something."

I roll my eyes. "Yeeesss… What?"

He looks at me and tilts his head.

"He said 'she's beautiful'."

I think of the way he responded, unhesitatingly matter of fact, and somehow it gets me just right. It is perfection. He gives me a crooked smile. I laugh. I take his hand and we head off to find a bar to talk about bad films.

Please

It is the middle, somewhere, between things gone before and things to come, breathless and stateless and suspended in a half-pause between want and need. Voices coloured with prickly desperation.

"Do you want me to fuck you?"

"Yes, I want you to fuck me Ma'am"

"I didn't hear you say please."

"Please Ma'am, please fuck me, please please please please please…"

Second one nighter

He was Clark Kent, tall and built and conservative, with glasses. Sweetly attentive, a combination of youthful cocky and shy insecurity. More than ten years younger, he had lied about his age.

"I thought you wouldn't be interested if you knew how young I was," he confessed later.

I had taken him home some weeks before, after a formal function, a night of drinking, dancing, flirting, and later fumbling one-night sex, hot and steamy and awkward, with bodies slamming and urgent whispered instructions punctuating other wordless sounds.

I had not spoken to him since, I was not interested, but tonight, at the event, I spotted him out of the corner of my eye, chatting by the bar, laughing with friends. The evening was lots of fun—drinks, food, laughs, enjoyable company and somewhere in there, without a word, without any contact, without even a glance, the hunger grew.

I decided.

I walked past his group on my way out, his back was to me. I tapped his elbow, he turned, mid chuckle at something someone had said. I looked up at him. He smiled, expecting chit chat, a hello at least.

"You coming?" I said.

I watched his face shift, shock registering the words, he was immediately flustered, I could almost feel his heart thumping at me, his cock hardening. I turned and walked away.

I heard him behind me, he stumbled over some words to his friends.

"I have to go…" he said in there somewhere.

I strolled down the stairs. Hailed a cab.

My orgasm

What I do love, do, and love, is to make him look into my eyes when he comes because it's mine, his orgasm... I want to get inside him and take it from him, to experience it with him, to see it in his eyes, his acknowledgement that it's mine, to feel his surrender of it to me.

Music festival

It's hot, sun beating down, the light dappled by leaves from overhanging trees.

You are dancing, your hair held up in a coloured band, it bounces wildly as you fling yourself about to the beat. You are lost in it. I feel wave after wave of affection as I watch you, unselfconscious, intermittently closing your eyes to let the music move you. My stomach flips when your lithe body does a snaky little shimmy that you will probably never do exactly like that again. I want to watch you do that move over and over, but it's gone.

I am silently urging you to take your t-shirt off. I know you will. Your fingers pluck at the hem of it, lifting it slightly to get some air onto your heated skin.

I watch young women sidle up beside you, swinging hips, opening their bodies to you. You smile widely at them, a smile of joy and welcome and camaraderie. I see them glow under it. I smile also because you seem unaware that they are mistaking your friendliness for something else. Right now, though, they are your people and all are a part of you.

One of the pretty young girls slips in very close, moving in time with you. The corners of your mouth turn down, for a moment you are puzzled. You reach out and your fingertips touch her hipbone. She thinks you are drawing her in and she sways her hips towards you to the beat. You hold firm, your fingers not yielding to her movements. You are stopping her from getting closer. I want to laugh, it amuses me to watch you navigate the bodies on offer. You hold her away from you for a moment until she figures it out and moves away.

You glance over at me, to check that I am watching. I am. Of course. I see your face soften under my gaze, the music trance momentarily broken and now you are dancing for me. You swing your hips, make a little 'come hither' motion with your fingertips. I shake my head slightly and smirk at you. You laugh and shake your head back at me, raise your eyebrows. You hold my gaze, your body vibrating with the beat, you slip one hand up under your t-shirt, sliding your fingers up your abs, lifting the fabric to show me your muscles tensing and relaxing as you move.

I laugh out loud with the pleasure of it, unheard in the cacophony of music, and offer you applause. You do a little bow, and smirk at me, an invitation, a provocation. Without missing a beat, you grab the bottom of your t-shirt and pull it off, your slick body still moving with the music.

I feel like I do a cartoon-gasp, lust rising into my throat, my jaw clenched, my smile sucked into a silent 'oh' of shock. You see my reaction and for a moment you stand still in the sea of bodies, transfixed, neither of us are smiling any more.

I am drowning in it, struggling to breathe, my whole body tensely coiled and you are frozen, pinned into stillness by the way I am looking at you. I mouth a word at you, your nostrils flare, your mouth opens, I know your cock is hard.

Fuck.

Drawing out hurt

"Hands behind your head."

You comply quickly, and you wait.

"We're going to do something that we've done before, can you guess?" I ask, smiling.

We are new together, there aren't that many choices.

"No Ma'am," you reply quickly. You are nervous.

"The pegs." I grin at you.

You make a face at me, screw up your nose, your lip curls. You are not into pain. In fact, you don't like it at all, the pegs are torturous for you.

"Shirt off, jeans off. Leave your boxers on."

You comply quickly and stand in front of me in your boxers, hands clasped again behind your head.

It's like every time is the first time I have seen your body and god, it makes my skin, my teeth, my mouth ache with want. You are so beautiful. I close my eyes and take a deep breath.

The desire to touch you makes me faint. I stroke your soft skin, my fingertips tracing the undulations caused by your lean muscle. Your nipples harden under my probing fingers, I touch your cock through your boxers, feeling it respond to me, running a palm over your arse, bringing my mouth to the curve of your shoulder to lick it gently. I stroke you like you are a racehorse, your skin quivers as I run my hands over it.

"Kneel," I say, and you drop to your knees. I grab your hair and pull you into the bedroom, you scramble awkwardly behind me.

"You know how this goes, right?"

You look up at me and nod. "Yes Ma'am, a peg, lots of pain, another peg, more pain, lots of swearing... I remember."

I laugh. "Sounds about right."

"Kneel on the edge of the bed," I command.

You quickly climb onto the bed and kneel there, hands again clasped behind your head. You are so fucking sexy waiting there, I want to push you back and just shove my cunt into your mouth. The thought makes my breath catch, and I let my head fill with it as I look at you.

I wave the pegs at you, smirking. You tilt your head at me, trying not to look concerned.

I press against you as you kneel there, and bring my mouth to yours, long, slow, leisurely kisses, like our mouths are fucking. I moan gently into your mouth and feel your hips push into me at the sound. I run my hands down your back and slip my fingers into your boxers to feel your arse, pull you harder against me. You make a soft grunting sound that goes straight to my cunt. I reach between us and close my fingers around your cock through your boxers and squeeze.

You push into my hand and the movement of your hips and the feel of your cock makes my pussy ache.

I pull reluctantly away from your mouth, my lips sliding down to your neck. I grip your hair and move your head to the side to stretch your neck as I kiss it, biting it hard, feeling you flinch, a groan escaping your lips.

I move down your chest to your left nipple. I lick it, suck it into my mouth, nibbling at it, then lapping gently with the flat of my tongue. I close my teeth around your flesh and pull at it, applying some pressure. It's hard. I grab the peg and pull the skin of your nipple forward, closing the peg on it.

I watch your face register the pain, my stomach flipping over as you bite your lip. You are trying to be stoic. I wait for you to swear.

"...Fucking fuck fuck..."

I grab your head and pull your mouth to mine, wanting to swallow your words, I kiss you aggressively and your angry mouth returns the kiss hard, taking my breath. So fucking hot, I'm making soft inarticulate noises into your mouth.

I release the kiss and bring my mouth to your right nipple, nip at it, sucking it hard, playing my teeth across it until I feel it harden on my tongue. I grab the second peg and gently, slowly close it on your nipple.

I step back and watch your face as you struggle with the pain. You are taking fast shallow breaths, your eyes closed.

I want to eat you up. I want to suck your cock while you are in this pain, I want to fuck you while you are in this pain, I want to fuck your mouth with my cunt while you are in this pain, I want you to beg for the pain so that I will not stop playing with you.

I move close to you again, watching your face as I snake my hand down your stomach, tracing the top of your boxers, my fingers creeping below the waistband.

"How does it feel, boy?" I ask.

"It fucking hurts...!" you snarl.

"It fucking hurts WHAT?" I snap back.

"It fucking hurts MA'AM!" you spit.

I stifle a laugh.

My hand finds your cock inside your boxers and I stroke it once to the tip and run my fingers over it to see if you are wet. I find some pre-come and withdraw my hand, bringing my fingers to your lips.

"Lick it."

You open your mouth I wipe my fingers on your tongue. You suck my fingers into your mouth and I feel your tongue lapping at them, just as they would lap at my cunt. I rest my other hand against the outline of your cock, a slight pressure.

"When I take the pegs off, this stops," I say, and wait for the thought to sink in, your face still contorting with pain.

"Fuck... fuucckking fuck," you mutter.

"Do you want me to take the pegs off, boy, you want this to stop?"

My fingertips play lightly against the straining fabric of your boxers, I feel more wetness.

"No, no leave them on Ma'am."

"Beg me to leave them on." I idly stroke your cock through your boxers.

"Please Ma'am, please please leave the pegs on, please Ma'am."

"Do you want to see how wet this makes me?"

"Yes, yes please Ma'am, please..."

I slowly undo my jeans, and pull them down a little while you watch. You can see my lacy g-string and you watch intently as my fingers disappear into my panties. I close my eyes as they find my clit, I linger there. With a soft moan, I slide them down into my wetness. I gather the moisture on my fingers, slipping them inside me.

I offer my glistening fingers up for you to see. You open your mouth, your tongue is already out, reaching for my fingers.

"Do you want to taste me, boy?"

"Yes, please please please please please, yes..."

You moan, leaning forward to reach my fingers.

I touch my fingers to your lips, you reach for them greedily with your tongue and I slide them into your mouth, feeling you lapping at them. I fuck your mouth gently with my fingers, I lean forward to lick your lips as you suck, wanting to fuck your mouth with my tongue as well as my fingers, wanting more, wanting to get inside your mouth.

The wanting draws a moan from deep in my throat.

I touch the pegs with my other hand, moving them. You spit out my fingers.

"Fucking motherFUCKER..." you hiss.

God, you are so fucking hot.

"Does it hurt, baby?" I ask disingenuously. "Want me to take them off, or do you want to feel how wet this makes me?"

Your face contorts with pain and you pant, short sharp breaths through your teeth.

"Feel, please, I want to feel how wet you are, please Ma'am."

"Beg me to hurt you again, baby".

You clench your teeth and shake your head at me. "Fucking fucking... fuck!!"

I smile at you and move closer, my lips touching yours. "Come on baby, beg me to hurt you."

You glare at me. Shake your head again.

"Hurt me... please..." You snarl it through tightened lips.

I bring my mouth to your tortured left nipple and lap at it, moving the peg, letting some blood circulate. You grind your teeth and groan as the waves of pain hit you. I do the same to the other nipple, lapping at it with my tongue, the movement excruciatingly painful.

I stand up and take one of your hands from behind your head and guide it down to my undone jeans. You don't hesitate, shoving your hand down into my panties, your fingers immediately sliding into wetness, touching it elicits a moan from the back of your throat. I catch my breath as you circle my clit, slick and slippery and I fuck my hips against the pressure. You slide your fingers further and your whole hand is covered in my wetness.

"Slide your fingers into my cunt," I whisper.

Your fingers slide easily inside me and I rock against the heel of your hand against my clit. I kiss you hard, sucking your tongue into my mouth, making a low sound that disappears down your throat. I fuck against your fingers, my mouth on yours, and feel you pulling me closer, trying to get contact with your cock.

I smile into your mouth and pull away, your hand slips out of my pants and you groan in disappointment.

I push you backwards onto the bed, and straddle you. I direct your wet hand to your mouth and tell you to lick it. I lean in close to watch your tongue lapping at your fingers, you deliberately do it slow, with long strokes, knowing it will drive me wild. I see the side of your mouth curling up into a half smile as you lick between your fingers, the pain momentarily forgotten as you tease me.

I watch your face closely as I reach for the first peg and flick it off. Your smile disappears, your mouth opens in protest, you grunt loudly. "FUCK!!!" You smack your head back into the bed over and over.

"Did I tell you to stop licking?" I ask.

"No Ma'am, but it fucking hurt...!!!" You see my look and you shut up, your tongue returning to its task.

You are waiting for the second peg to be removed now, you wince in anticipation each time I move, your face screwed up as you lick at your fingers. I lean down and kiss you, softly gentle, tasting myself on your tongue, you open up to me and I nudge at your mouth for more. I wait until you start to kiss me back before I reach for the second peg and slowly, gently open it. The blood returning to it radiates hot pain and I keep my mouth on yours as you groan from the hurt.

You moan your pain into my mouth, it makes me ravenous for you, I swallow it down as my fingers find your nipple and you squirm under me as I draw out more.

Why chastity?

For me, the why:

Because it's so fucking HOT!

Because it's extended foreplay.

Because it is fascinating to watch how it impacts him.

Because his arousal makes me wet, so more is better.

Because it's sexual torture.

Because he's so fucking beautiful when he's hard and denied.

Because everything turns him on when he's in that state.

Because it's hellishly fun.

Because his cock is mine and I can.

Did I mention it's fucking HOT?!

Oh. My. Fucking. God: HOT!!!

Yogacam

The agreement is clearly laid out: He will get on cam and do half an hour of yoga. He will do it shirtless. We will not speak beforehand. I will initiate the call at the agreed time. He will turn the webcam on, I will verify by IM that I can see, and he will begin. He is to pretend I am not watching. No mugging for the cam, no sly smiles, no showing off.

He has never been on cam for me, though I have seen him already in photos and video clips that he has sent me over the time we have been talking.

He is beautiful.

A mane of thick black hair frames an angular face: full well-defined lips, a cheeky smile, and expressive brown eyes come together to form an impression of open boyish curiosity. He has a lean tight build, sinewy muscled arms, a washboard stomach all rippled and shapely, and slim little hips that flare out into smooth broad pecs.

I could hardly think of anything more insanely voyeuristically hot than watching this beautiful man do yoga for me.

I Skype him at the agreed time, a glass of champagne by my hand.

The webcam flickers and comes to life.

He is standing a little to the left, I see the side of his half-naked body, then he bends down and peers nervously into the camera, a smile, then I am treated to a close up of his six packed stomach as he stands back up in front of the computer, waiting for me to verify that it is working. I am already distracted by the curves of his smooth skin so close and untouchable, I can see his gentle breaths rippling across his abdominal muscles as he waits not a few inches away from my view.

I message him. "Okay, move back so I can see where you will be doing the yoga."

He steps away from the cam so that I can see into the space he has set up. A candle burns in a Buddha statue in the corner, a green yoga mat clearly in view, a mirror on the wall.

"Yes, perfect."

He steps into the room, self consciously walks over to the mat, and stands still for a moment, focussing, perhaps giving me a leisurely moment to look at him at rest. His hands come together as if in prayer and he reaches up to salute the sun, the skin of his torso pulls taut across his ribs, his waist becomes a tiny touchable wisp, his back arches as he stretches.

I smile and take a sip of champagne.

On kissing you

It is gentle, this image I have of kissing you, soft and exploratory.

Maybe because you are so naively greedy, offering yourself with no real clue what you are putting on the table. You think you can give it because you don't know any better.

It would be tender: a slow approach, watching your reaction, seeing the longing, the yearning, the guileless reaching. It is heartbreaking, really, the innocence of it, the trust. And oh my god, the shy hesitance, accentuated by the bottomless eagerness, the wide-eyed artless desire.

I know you would sink quickly under the onslaught I ache to enact on you, but that's not what I want.

I want you to come to me.

I want to wait within an inch of your reach, my eyes on your face, my tongue slipping out to touch my top lip, your gaze fixated on that small flickering movement, waiting for my mouth. I will linger there for as long as it takes for you to give in and come to me.

Come to me, baby... yes, just like that.

You reach for me, closing the gap between us, your mouth soft, lips parted, your eyes closing in anticipation.

You don't get to kiss me though... no no... too easy.

I pull back from you and watch your face, your eyes flicker open at being denied, confusion, hurt... I see you wonder silently. "Isn't this what you wanted?"

Oh yes, baby, yes it's what I wanted, exactly what I wanted...but it's not enough, I want more. That's too easy, and I always want more.

I adore your bewilderment, that puzzled look on your face, that slight fear that you have done something wrong, it breaks my heart even as it makes me wet.

You are waiting now. Anxious that you have done the wrong thing, you are made hesitant.

And now I get to touch your lips with mine, to stroke against you, and I know you will pause there, your breath quickening, you will melt into my touch, and wait, giving me free reign. My tongue slipping between your lips, pulling your full, pillowy-soft bottom lip towards me, that warm wet slickness making me want to grab you by the hair and smash into you, but I don't.

I am so fucking gentle with you that it makes my insides clench with the impossible restraint of it, a groan of frustration escapes me. I am fighting the urge to crash hard into you, to shove you to the ground, to bite your mouth and slap your face, to see your stunned shock in it, to see you reach desperately for the violence of my kiss. I want it so badly, your surrender under this assault, but I hold it all back, muscles trembling with the suppressed desire.

Instead, I part your lips so gently with mine that it barely feels like we are touching, and I feel you give under it, sensitive to every slight movement. You open your mouth to me and invite me in, my tongue reaching for yours, tentative, exploratory. I feel your greed for more, you are holding back also, pretending to be a passive recipient, but I can taste this pent up energy coiled in waiting, flavours of blood and iron. I feel it in your desperate breaths, in your tight muscles, clenched fists, that strangled sound in the back of your throat.

I curb every aggressive instinct in me and instead tease out the leisurely moments with you like this, shuddering breaths shared between us revealing the strain of holding back. The excruciating pleasure of these slow moments of connection stretch out forever, and longer, until there is nothing except this second of intense intimacy, and then the next.

Public tease

A concert, it's dark. I'm there with my girlfriends. Crowded at the front, squeezed together, heat, and a pounding beat through the floor. Bodies moving in unison, we are all one undulating, connected creature, for a brief moment, strangers bonded together.

I feel him behind me, pressed up against me in the throng. He is tall, I don't turn around, but graze my arse back a little against him. I feel him retreat away from me politely. I allow it, until a surge towards the stage returns him to me. I dance back against him, feel him try to pull his hips away from the contact, but there is nowhere for him to go. He thinks it's unintentional, is trying not to be a creep. I love him a little for this, with the music pounding in my head and my body answering the beat.

I feel the front of his jeans, rough fabric through my thin skirt. It slips against my arse every time I sway my hips, a gentle touch in time to the drum bass, I know he is still wondering if it's an accident. He stops trying to move away, instead he keeps still while everyone around him is dancing. I feel him trying not to be pushed by the crowd, he wants to know if I am doing this on purpose, he waits for me to touch him.

The music is maddening, my dancing loose and free and through it, I feel his stillness there behind me. I push back against him over and again and now he stands his ground, feet braced, waiting there for me. I rub against him and feel his hips move with me now. Hellishly hot, I feel him trying to fit against me, to manoeuvre himself so that I am unhindered in my efforts to grind back against him.

A slow song, the crowd softens, sways, I lean back into him, gently move against him in time to the music, my arse pressed firmly into his groin, his hips nudge forward. I slip against him to the beat, and he moves with me, this time no pretence at propriety, I feel his cock harden against my arse, he rests a cheek against my hair. His cock is deliciously insistent, I stroke the length of it with my arse as I swing my hips rhythmically to the music, he tries to keep beat with me for maximum contact. The song seems to go on forever, and his fingers slip gently along the side of my body, down to my waist, my hip, he wants to feel me, to pull me back against him, he wants more. I shove his hand away, that's not how this game works. He recoils, as if he has been scalded, and I feel his hesitation, he waits to see if I will end this thing we are sharing. I don't.

When the beat picks up again, I feel him behind me trying to make himself available, trying to anticipate which way I will move so he can move with me. A strange dance between strangers, made hot with the crashing, stroking, rubbing of bodies in the heat of the public setting.

I don't remember now who the band was or what friends I was with, but I remember him. I spent the entire concert with the amazing hotness of this anonymous contact, being incredibly aroused by this stranger whose face I never saw, pretending to ignore him while teasing him madly. I never turned around, never acknowledged his existence, and after the band played their last song, I strode away with my friends without looking back.

Afterwards, kissing

I love to kiss him when he is endorphined and blissed, when everything in him is made soft and his eyes are glazed. He would be happy to lie there with me and float away, but when I touch his cheek he turns to face me, not really looking, not really, he is elsewhere, but I know he feels the feather-like touch through the haze.

His mouth is made so gentle when he is like this, his lips cushiony-soft and relaxed, and sometimes his tongue slips out to touch the tender skin there, abused and sore. In this state, he is innocent of the impact it has, the gesture oddly childlike.

If I pet his cheek, bring my face closer, he comes back, blinks slowly, and focuses on me, and in his look I see myself reflected back. In this moment, I am all the gods of fear and violence, and I am beauty and love and I swear that if I pushed a little harder, he would cry, or I would, perhaps both.

I touch my lips to his and I feel him shift into it, soft grazing touches, so as not to shock him out of his pillowy dream, his mouth slack at first, accepting and giving. I pull his face to me and slide closer to him, wanting his hot wet skin against me. He starts to shift to meet me, and we move together, scissoring our legs, and I make one fluid movement into him, to bring our hips together, to fit into him, to touch him everywhere, I wrap his head in my arms, tilt his face up to me.

And when I bring my mouth to his again, it is like we have never kissed before, like it is the first time over and over. He makes small sounds of wonder and aching desire, even though he is still not there with me. My mouth explores his lips gently, my tongue lapping at him softly, a foray into his dreamy state, and his surrender feels like drifting down into the depths of a quiet dark lake.

He whispers a tiny, "Please" at me, and I know he is asking for anything and everything, and nothing, all at the same time.

I whisper "Yes" into his mouth in a kiss and he sighs contentedly and melts himself into me.

Dirty secrets

She smirked across the table at him.

He laughed. "What?!"

She raised an eyebrow. "I beg your pardon?"

He looked puzzled, then gave her a sheepish smile. "What are you thinking, Ma'am?"

She eyed his crotch, then looked back up to his face.

His eyes widened, brow furrowed.

"Your lap," she said, as if it wasn't obvious.

Understanding dawned. He hesitated, then shifted his chair back, the feet scraping loudly on the floor, he didn't look around to see if anyone noticed. He leaned back in the seat, grinned cockily at her, looked pointedly at his crotch, then back at her.

She laughed. In a swift move, she stood, slid over and settled herself in his lap.

She shuffled to get more comfortable. He pulled her close, one arm going around her back, the other landing gently on her thigh, stroking her leg through the light fabric of her skirt.

She wrapped an arm around his neck, leaning into him. She grabbed her wine off the table, took a sip and offered it to his mouth. He parted his lips and she tipped the glass to let the cold clear liquid flow onto his tongue, watching intently as he swallowed.

"Lick it," she whispered into his ear.

She watched his tongue, moistly tipped, flatten and swipe the edge of the glass slowly, his eyes looking up at her.

She made a low sound of pleasure and felt him stiffen under her.

She brought her lips to rest against his ear, breathed softly into it. "Good boy, I like it when you do that..."

"Yes Ma'am," he whispered, his eyes glazing over.

He tilted his head to give her better access to his ear, he loved her voice, low and gentle, her mouth against him. He half closed his eyes.

She chuckled softly at his reaction, feather-light exhalations against his skin.

She whispered, "You want me to tell you some secrets, boy?"

His lips curled upwards into a smile, he took a deep breath.

"Yes, please Ma'am."

She contemplated him, had another sip of wine. She tilted his head up to her, brought her lips to his and let the cool liquid slip into his mouth. She followed with a kiss before he could swallow, her fingers curling around his neck to hold him there. He tried to quickly down the wine and kiss her back at the same time, reaching for her just as she pulled away.

She squirmed in his lap. He sank down a little lower in his seat, enjoying her weight moving against him. He held his breath, waiting.

She brought her mouth back to his ear. "Secrets?"

He exhaled, nodded.

"Please, Ma'am," he said softly.

She thought for a moment. Then she lowered her lips back to his ear, her warm breath against him, and she started quietly telling him dark, dirty, terrifying, wonderful secrets, her lips occasionally grazing his sensitive skin, her breath delivering each word directly to his core.

There's something about him

We have a short phone call at 11.30pm, so I can tell him a bedtime story.

We talk about trivialities: my stubbed toe, his dog hair problem, wine...

I listen to him brush his teeth, a domestic intimacy.

He calls me 'sweetie', it is... well, sweet.

We talk and joke about nothing much at all.

I ask him later if he is already in bed. He says he is, of course. We talk some more.

Time for the bedtime story.

I tell him to get out of bed, to kneel by it, and to ask me if he can get into it.

It surprises him. It is the first time I have asked anything like this of him.

I hear him shift, a deep breath, I can almost taste it. He makes a sound as if he is reeling, it is quite lovely.

He gets out of bed, and gently asks if he can please get into bed. I can hear that he is turned on by it.

I say yes, and thank him for it, amused and aroused by this small gesture.

He tells me through a smile that he is hard now. I have not made it a rule yet, but I like it when he tells me... it is hot to hear him say it out loud.

"Also... no touching your cock while I am reading to you..."

He groans at that. "Okay..."

"Pardon?"

"Okay Ma'am, yes Ma'am."

"That's what I thought you said..."

He checks again. "No touching at all?"

"None, unless I say you can, which is unlikely..."

"Yes Ma'am, that seems unlikely."

I tell him to shush then.

I read a hot story I wrote about us to him. He makes small inarticulate sounds in my ear as I read to him in a low soft voice.

I allow him to touch himself for two sentences worth, twice. He thanks me and his tone gets a different tenor, lower, concentrated. His voice in my ear makes my stomach flip over.

I tell him to stop when the two sentences are done.

When I finish the reading, I pause for a moment, then say goodnight, and hang up.

When I get off the phone, I slip a finger down to my pussy. I am so fucking wet, my finger slips easily between my lips, completely slick. Just from that. I come about 5 minutes after the phone call ends.

Sexual violence

I will like it if you can be stunned into weakness for me, when I can shove you into a wall, a hand around your throat and threaten you and have you believe it (crossing that line between knowing that you can stop it any time you want and that tipping over point where the attack makes your brain stutter and your body go 'wtf?!'). If I am aggressively fucking with you, I need to believe that you are in it with me, that when I slap you or bite you, you have some fear that I am going to lose it and rip the flesh from your bones. I want you to be afraid, and maybe it is a fear of doing or saying the wrong thing more than a physical fear, and that works too: I want to taste it, fear and confusion and desire.

If I can get there, this is my favourite, all messy and violent, and there will be bruises that don't come from some careful wielding of a nicely crafted flogger. I will be rabid for wanting to get inside your skin, clawing at it like it's in the way and kissing, your mouth will hurt from it, from me trying to rip your tongue from you and swallow it, from biting at your lips because they are mine and shouldn't even be on your fucking face. Shoving your face into the floor and resisting the urge to smash it into the hardness over and over again, grinding relentlessly against parts of your body that are in my fucking way and stopping me from getting inside you. I can't get enough, I know it already, but I will want to tear you apart trying.

Then at some point, I have to come back from that because it only goes so far, and when I come back from it, I want to see you bared, open and looking a little lost, reeling from it. Hard and desperate and put upon, and I will be melting from what you have given me under the onslaught, and from you being just a little bit broken. I want that lost boy who blinks up at me, vulnerable and open now, like everything inside has spilled out because his mind was so busy processing what was going on that it had to leave the reason-driven part of him behind.

And then I get to play with you, that wide-eyed boy, with gentleness and hints of hurt that now make you a little scared, that hit you hard because you think it is done now, because you are already sore and think you maybe can't take any more: it makes me both protective and predatory. And I let you see how turned on this makes me, all of it. And maybe I blame you for that "See what you did?!" and slap you and maybe let you taste it. And maybe you get to lick me with the remnants of violence on us both, then it is more like sex with lots of kissing and teasing and denial and some sharpness just to remind you I am there, and maybe the strap-on and maybe cuffs and gags and blindfolds and licking and general fuckery.

Face fuck

You in a darkened room, alone, tied up.

Hands together, ankles together.

You are kneeling.

You are waiting.

And waiting.

The door opens.

Light from the room beyond blinds you; seems you have been there quite a while.

You squint, shield your eyes, see a silhouette, that's all.

The door closes, dark again.

You hear three long strides and you are shoved backwards from your kneel.

Your tied hands are pulled up over your head, you shuffle as you are dragged backwards. You try to follow the tugging at your arms, unsure what you are supposed to do.

The hands pull you back towards the floor, you shift quickly to lie on your back. A kick to your side causes you to exhale sharply, shock more than hurt.

A weight on your chest, warm, someone sitting on you.

You smell pussy.

A hand grips your hair tightly, pulls your head up off the floor.

Someone moans, maybe it's you.

Thighs on either side of your head.

Your mouth already open, tongue out.

A cunt lowers onto your mouth, slides against your lips.

You lap, bury your tongue in the folds, a musky rich scent fills your nostrils. You play softly and gently at licking, your lips nuzzle against the wetness. Your hair is pulled hard to move your head where it needs to go. You lick whatever is in front of your mouth. You find her clit, you suck it into your mouth.

You hear a gasp.

Your head is smacked back into the floor, you grunt.

A casual blow to your cheek. Your head rocks to the side.

You whisper a silent apology.

Another blow regardless.

You whimper.

Lick your lips, stick your tongue out again.

Her cunt lowers onto your face.

The taste again makes you moan into her.

She moves against you. You try and pick up her rhythm. Her weight gets heavier against your face, you take little breaths when you can.

You make your tongue flat, feeling the smoothness of her labia slick against you. She slides against your tongue, splitting her cunt with it, pausing as you hit her clit.

You stick your tongue out further, offering, to see if she wants to fuck it. You try desperately to fuck her with it, to stick your tongue into her.

Your face covered in wetness, you gasp for air when she gives you space.

She lifts a little, you feel her clit against your lips, try to get the right angle to lap at it. You flick your tongue against it.

You hear her make a sound far above you, you lick right there.

Your tongue now knows where to flick and tries to find that spot over and again. She pulls you into her, smothering your face with her cunt. She bucks against you, the grip in your hair keeping your mouth hard up against her.

She fucks your face relentlessly, like it's a thing she got to fuck.

Finally, the rocking gets faster, the pressure against your mouth almost unbearable.

You struggle to breathe.

The grip in your hair excruciatingly tight, hair pulled out by the roots.

You feel thigh muscles tensing against your head.

Keeping your tongue right there, on that spot.

She fucks your face thoughtlessly, short hard strokes. You can't breathe, your body starts to rebel against it.

She suddenly makes a lot of noise, pulls your face hard up into her pussy, squeezes her thighs around your head. Your face smashes into her cunt, mouth open, trying to breathe. She bucks against you, unconscious final spasms, slowing.

The grip in your hair loosens, you get a sliver of space.

You suck in air desperately, gasping loudly.

You hear her sigh.

She lets go of your hair, your head falls back to the floor with a thump. She wipes the slick wetness of her cunt on your chest.

The weight lifts from your body.

You hear footsteps walking away from you.

The door opens, a flash of light, then gone as the door shuts again.

You are alone, in the dark.

Waiting.

Rubbing myself raw

I rubbed myself raw on him.

We have a word here: pashing. Do you know it? It's snogging, making out. It's origin is 'passionate', which of course makes it a word I love, even though it is an old term from my adolescence and rather out of favour. "Pash rash" is the irritation you get around your mouth if you have done a lot of pashing, most common on women because men may have rough skin or stubble.

In this case, I got more of a gravel rash, even though I had him shaving twice a day. The skin around my mouth was red, but my chin, constantly rubbing against him, was abraded, scraped of skin, then scraped some more, to the point of bleeding.

I couldn't get enough of him, even when it was clear it was damaging me, when it got to the point where it hurt me to kiss him.

And still, more kissing please...

UNDER HIS CLOTHES

She placed a palm on his chest, the warmth of her hand a reassurance through his t-shirt. She felt bulky muscle, strong, shapely.

She was surprised, gently shocked, she looked at him. He looked thinner, softer than the body she felt hidden from her under his clothes.

She ran her hand over his pecs, reassurance turned to curiosity to feel what lay beneath the fabric.

Fingertips travelled over surprisingly firm muscle, a well defined chest, she ran her fingers along the curved ridge of his ribs, then cruised back up, feeling the bump of his nipples as she slid nails gently over them, curiosity tipping into unashamedly enjoying the feel of him.

She cocked her head at him.

"You have a beautiful chest, I don't understand why you are shy about taking your shirt off," she murmured softly.

He responded awkwardly, shifting quietly, eyes downcast.

She took hold of the bottom of this t-shirt, tugged at it. He raised his hands obediently into the air, she smiled.

Another drink?

I glance sideways at you, catch your eye. You are watching me. I know that look, it says "Here I am, Ma'am...", it invites and challenges me, it waits.

I smirk at you, watch you blush. I know you want to look away now that you have caught my attention. Now that you have what you want you aren't quite sure what to do with it.

I turn to face you and you hold your breath, steel yourself, shore yourself up. Oh my fucking god, so unbearably hot. It tugs at my cunt, makes my heart thump in my chest, makes my stomach lurch.

Your mouth lifts into a half smile, I watch your lips curl, you shift on the bar stool, your fingers plucking at your jeans, trying to hold my gaze.

"Another drink?" you ask, nodding at my empty glass.

I shake my head, shift slightly and slip off my seat. The move brings me six inches closer to you, I touch your knee, you inhale, not quite a gasp, then exhale slowly.

I tilt my head at you, your face turns into a question mark as I step closer. I apply some pressure to your knee with my thigh, make you widen your legs a little more, you spread them, give me room to step between them. I shake my head slightly, too wide, you shift again, trying to figure out what I want. I nod when you get it right.

I slowly scrunch my skirt up with my right hand, feeling it slip up over my knee, gathering the material in my fingers, it slides up my thigh until I have a handful of fabric in my hand and my right leg is exposed. I stand on my toes, my calves contracting, my stiletto heels lift an inch off the floor.

I take a step forward, my bare leg slipping between your denimed thighs, I slide my panty clad pussy along your leg, keeping the fabric of my skirt to one side, feeling the roughness of your jeans against my skin, through the silk at my crotch.

You make a strangled sound as I straddle your leg and slide forward against your thigh, I drop the skirt to conceal what I am doing, squirm against you, feel the heat of my pussy warming your leg. I grab a handful of your hair at the back of your head, to steady myself. I position myself on your thigh, and rock almost imperceptibly against you. You shuffle forward a little to give me better access, I know you want to pull me tight against you, I see your grip on the bar tense, your knuckles whiten.

I tighten my thigh and arse muscles to create some friction against you, a sensuous, slow, subtle movement... contracting and releasing, grinding hard and slow on your leg. My breathing changes, becomes deeper, heavy, as I shift slightly to get the angle and pressure I want, silk against denim, hot and humid, slick. You are crackling with energy, every muscle tight, I can feel your desire to push forward, to get more contact, I don't have to look to know that your cock is hard, as if reading my thoughts you shift again, exhale through gritted teeth, make small sounds in the back of your throat.

I tighten my fist in your hair and tilt your head, bring your face close to mine, your mouth inches away, I breathe against you, watching your face. You strain against my grip to get at me, open your mouth slightly, your tongue slips out, wets your lips, I feel your strength, I hear what sounds like a whimper.

I am unhurried, pressing myself against you like you are some public masturbation tool placed there for my convenience. My movements are almost imperceptible, and I feel you trying to give me what I want, your breathing uneven, I wonder if your jeans are getting wet and resist the urge to slip my hand down to feel the spot where I am connected to you.

Finally I manoeuvre your head to one side awkwardly, forcing your ear close to my lips, my voice low, a whisper.

"Let's go, boy."

You lean your cheek against mine, your breathing quick and shallow, you moan softly.

I take that as a "yes Ma'am."

Boy under her heels

She has on her new ankle boots, black leather, stiletto heels, stockings... she has them on, at home, in the house. His eyes are wide as he takes in the clingy black dress, the red lipstick. On the table, water crackers and various cheeses; brie, camembert, vintage cheddar, what looks like Edam. She is leaning back comfortably in the black leather swivel chair, legs crossed, a boot swinging hypnotically back and forth. She has a glass of white wine in her hand.

She snaps her fingers, points to the floor in front of her. He is kneeling at her feet within seconds, no longer smiling, he is attentive, waiting, he looks up at her with that expression on his face, the one that makes her stomach flip over with its open desire.

"Hello Ma'am," he says, quietly.

They talk about inconsequential things, she sips her wine, watching his lips move as he tells her about his day. She brings her boots to rest on his thighs, leans forward, the heels digging in a little, she watches him concentrate on speaking to her. She nods occasionally, starts to undo the buttons of his shirt, pulls at him to bring him closer, his talk slows.

She asks him questions, random, irrelevant ones as

she tugs at the shirt. He tries to answer. She shuffles her thigh-resting boots closer to his crotch, applies pressure as she leans forward to push the shirt back off his shoulders. Sees him wince as the heels dig into him, the shirt drops to the floor. He tries to keep the conversation going, becoming more and more distracted.

The t-shirt underneath is untucked quickly, she pulls at it, loves how he lifts his arms up for her so that she can take it off him, it is a childlike innocence, it never fails to make her throat tighten.

She sits back, takes a sip of wine, his talk trails off, they look at each other.

She crooks her finger at him in a 'come-hither' motion, widens her legs so that he can get closer, in between them. He shuffles forward. She places a finger under his chin and pushes upward, he tilts his head back, sees her scowl, she sees the 'tick-tick' of his nervous brain work out what she wants and he lifts his arse off his heels and kneels up. She nods slightly in response, he half smiles at her.

She undoes his leather belt, fumbles at the buttons of his jeans, his breath quickens, his hips tense. She tries not to smile, takes her time, deliberately slow, unnecessarily awkward, she rests her cheek against his, breathes softly in his ear, resists the urge to kiss him, but rubs against his face instead, kitten-like, insistent, feels him lean into her to increase the contact.

She pushes his jeans down off his hips, plants a boot at the crotch of them and shoves them to the floor. His cock now straining against his dark grey boxer briefs, she brushes the back of her hand against the hardness, feels wet fabric as her cool skin passes gently over it.

She pulls the waist of his boxers away from his body, slides it over his cock, letting her fingers trail against his skin as she slips them down, again with the boot in the crotch to push them to the floor.

"Take them off," she says.

He stands up quickly, she smirks at the jeans and boxers crumpled at his knees, watches him, resists the urge to take his cock in her fist and hear his reaction if she were to give it one, two hard vicious strokes. He blushes, as if he has played her thoughts in his head, slips off his shoes and socks quickly, steps out of his pants, in seconds he is naked, kneeling up between her legs again.

She sits on the edge of the seat, pulls her skirt up to her thighs, her stockinged legs bared, she wraps them around him, resting her spiky heels on his calves. She moves against him, the silky fabric of her thighs sliding against the sides of his body, her stockinged calves slipping against his arse, the softness contrasting with the sharp edge of her heels scraping his skin. He gazes up at her with rapt attention, she watches his eyes glaze over, he has a thing for stockings that he doesn't quite understand, he is unsteady, his hips twitching, wanting... something. She brings one leg back to the front, rubs against his cock and slides it firmly between his thighs, the fabric slipping against his cock and balls, he holds his breath, tries to stay still, makes a choked moaning sound when she repeats the movement.

She snaps her fingers, points again to the hardwood floor.

"Lie down, on your back."

He slides inelegantly to the floor at her feet. She nudges him into the position she wants with the toe of her boot.

She rests her boots on his stomach. The heels are sharp around the edges, they scrape, will cut easily, they are different kinds of dangerous than just the stiletto points. She drags them across the sensitive skin, he closes his eyes, shifts uneasily, she watches the scratch marks appear, digs a little deeper, feels him tense under her, a sound escapes his lips. She crisscrosses his stomach with her heels, scratching, digging, twisting. He makes small whimpering sounds.

She picks up her glass, takes a sip of wine and scrapes her heels down towards his cock, she smirks as it twitches, sees his muscles tighten. She slides a toe of the boot under his cock and brings her other down on top of it, trapping it between them, her heels dig into his thigh and she allows the weight of her legs to rest on him.

She relaxes now, leans back, carefully chooses some soft brie, places it on a cracker and slips it into her mouth.

She savours the creamy taste, makes a sound of pleasure.

"Mmmmmmm..."

She feels his cock move against the bottom of her boot, reacting to her voice, she squeezes it in response, feels his hips rise. She leisurely chooses a different cheese, sinks back in her seat, each movement reflected against his cock, he moans softly as the heel scrapes against his inner thigh, and his cock is stroked by her changing positions. She is unhurried, as one should be with good cheese. She talks to him softly about what she is eating, describing flavours and textures. She sips the wine.

BEDTIME STORY

We are on the phone. It is late. He is tired.

"Go and brush your teeth, get into bed, and I will read you a bedtime story."

He thinks I am joking. I'm not. After a few minutes, he is still talking to me... I interrupt him.

"Teeth, bed! Go on!"

He laughs softly with surprise. "Yes Ma'am!" and scrambles off to do just that. I hear him shuffling and moving about.

Presently he returns, scooches into bed, tells me that he's ready.

"I'm going to read you the story, then I am going to say goodnight, okay?"

"Okay... but... what if I fall asleep?"

I smile. "That's okay, it's a bedtime story!"

"Really, you won't think it's rude?"

"No!... Now, shhhh..."

He smiles... nods... settles into bed, snuffling and curling up.

I wait a moment for him to get comfortable, and begin to read.

I read softly to him, the story is fun, light, has childish rhymes in it that make me stifle a laugh. He snickers occasionally, snuggled up in bed, his eyes closed. I feel as if I am wrapping him up in it tenderly, lulling him to sleep, petting him.

"...The End," I say quietly when I finish. "Goodnight, sweet dreams..."

I hear a muffled and sleepy, "Goodnight... night..."

I hang up gently.

Good morning

It is morning, he is still asleep, I am reading in the lounge room, the bedroom door in my peripheral vision. He is not allowed to come out of the room without permission.

I hear a sound and lift my gaze, the smirk already curling the corners of my mouth. The door opens slowly, his hand appears curled around the jamb, he peeks around the corner at me like a naughty child, blinking into the sunlight slowly.

My stomach lurches at the sight of him like I have been punched, I want to groan with the power of it, I raise an eyebrow at him.

"Hello Ma'am," he murmurs, a sleepy smile on his face, he rubs one eye with his fist and the unselfconscious innocence of it undoes me.

I am on my feet in a heartbeat and it seems to take only two steps to cross the room to get to him, his mouth widens into a smile when he sees me coming and changes to an 'oh' of shock when I grab him and shove him backwards into the bedroom. I run at him with force and don't stop barrelling until he has tripped back onto the bed and lands with a thump.

He laughs with delight.

"Oh, I like this!" followed by an 'ooomph' of exhalation as I land on top of him.

His hands automatically lift above his head as if he is restrained, and he is somehow immediately melting into the bed, his surrender making his eyes glaze even as they lock onto mine. He reaches for me with his mouth, his naked body pushing up towards the weight of me on top of him, his cock hard and straining against my thigh.

My mouth smashes into him and my teeth clash against his, we both wince and I hold his head still while I try and climb into his open mouth, I feel him trying to open up for me and I am grabbing at his flesh and finally get into some awkward position where I can dig my fingernails into his nipples and make his body arch up off the bed and make him utter some sound that I have heard before and have never heard before as I try to rip his skin off his bones.

Rope play

He wears black boxer briefs, also a rope corselet in white, a rope pentagram harness in white and red, a collar, wrist and ankle cuffs, a ball gag, a blindfold, he is kneeling.

I clip his wrist cuffs to the rope at his belly, I examine the ties, the loops, the smoothness of the rope around him by touch, reach between his legs to pull the ends forward, through his legs and up to attach it to the d-rings on his collar. I pull it tight. I am petting him, exposed skin, my knee pressed against his groin.

I stroke the rope that slips around and around his body, tug on the knots to watch him react. I see something change when I put pressure on the rope attached to the collar and pull his face towards me. He reaches for me: I feel it awaken.

I pull his sightless face to me, his mouth stretched silently open around the ball gag. I touch my cheek to his gently, then explore his face softly with mine. His breathing changes with this intimacy. I brush his skin with my cheek, I nudge gently at his nose with my nose, I let my lip catch on his, he leans further in to me, moves his head to find me as I change positions, as if he would kiss me if he wasn't blind and mute. I can smell the desire in him rising, he shifts on his knees, a shuffle, leans further forward to reach for me, he is hard up against my knees now, I place a hand on his chest to stop him toppling over. His almost imperceptible movement, his unseeing search for more contact sharpens my focus, makes my heart beat a little faster.

I do this for a long time, travelling his face with mine, inhaling him, drinking in his reaction. It is a silent exploration, feather touches, tender, subtle, almost nothing at all. I can feel how it gets inside him, he is sending me waves of want, it crackles between us, it is a gentle and powerful hotness.

Finally I whisper in his ear, "How are you doing there?"

He tilts his head to press his cheek against mine, nods, and the moment slips away.

Introduction...

We have caught up three, maybe four times in the last few months. We eat, we drink, we talk. We have spent quite a few hours together, we get along well, but we are not a romantic relationship match.

He is a pretty boy, who thinks he is not. He doesn't look in the mirror and see who he is, but who he is not.

He has no experience, is scared, his trust in me is a gift, it feels tentative. As much as play with him is about me exploring some rope play, it is also about gentleness, warmth, safety.

I want him to come away feeling like he has been in a space with infinite possibilities, a starting point where the next step to reach some of them is doable and positive.

I want him to come away feeling better, stronger, more confident, perhaps to believe that what he seeks is okay, is achievable.

I want him to come away thinking that maybe he is that pretty boy, maybe, just a bit.

The proposition

"I have a proposition for you..."

He looks at me curiously, tilts his head.

"Oookkkaayy?"

I smile. "I'm thinking that I'd like to do some rope bondage with you."

He looks away from me, bondage is one of his kinks, he is a complete newbie, has no experience. He is suddenly shy, awkward, he smiles nervously, starts to say something.

I interrupt him. "Don't answer now, I want you to have a think about it."

He nods.

I try to draw a picture of how I see it going. "I am thinking of something very gentle, not sexual, no nudity..." I look him up and down. "... boxers..."

He nods again, smiles uncertainly, looks at me, then away again.

"I know that you really want to experience this within a relationship, romantic and all that, and I will not be at all offended if you don't want to..."

I let the thought trail off and look at him, I touch his arm, smile reassuringly, go on.

"I have no experience with it..." I smirk at him, the

guinea pig,"... so haven't a clue what I am doing, it will be slow and awkward, I will be reading instructions from a book, probably talking to myself, it will possibly be very boring..." I shrug a bit, not sure, really, how it will go.

"... or it might be a bit of a peaceful zen-like experience... but I get to practice some rope bondage, you get to be practiced on..."

He tells a little story then, of a submissive he saw, or heard about, who was bound, minor bondage... and from it, she came. He is confessing that he is not sure how he will react, at the very least, maybe, he will get turned on, he is worried that it is not allowed.

I smile at him warmly, he is terribly sweet.

"That's fine, of course! To be expected, it will be sensual, there will be touching, so naturally..."

He smiles at me, on edge, restless. We talk a little more then, about my lack of experience with rope, about some bondage books he has, about less intimate things, I know the idea thrills and frightens him. I am not sure which will win out.

"I'll definitely be in touch... about it." he says as we part.

I smile, nod, lean into a gentle hug, reach up to give him a soft kiss on the cheek, I make my way home.

Play list

The proposition leads to a yes leads to a discussion leads to a negotiation. I send him a play list. It lists all the activities that I may want to do with him.

It is not a 'will do' list. It is a 'might, possibly, maybe, if it feels right, these are in the realms of possibility' list.

He gets to rate them from 0 to 5, he gets to add to them, he gets to say 'No'.

0 means he has utterly no desire to do that activity and doesn't like doing it (in fact, may loathe it) and would ordinarily object to doing it, but he would do it if I really wanted it. 5 means the activity is a wild turn-on for him.

- Being left in bondage (5-10 minutes)
- Being undressed (to boxer briefs)
- Biting (gentle)
- Blindfold
- Collar (wearing)
- Eye contact restrictions (not allowed to raise eyes/look at something)
- Gag
- Kissing
- Kneeling

- Leash (being led)
- Leash (wearing)
- Photos (of rope work, not face)
- Physical inspection
- Pinching (gentle)
- Being restrained (eg wrist/ankle cuffs tied to something)
- Rope bondage (ha!)
- Using honorific (Ma'am)
- Voice restrictions (not allowed to talk)
- Wearing ankle cuffs
- Wearing wrist cuffs

I send it to him.

Then I wait.

An Invitation

If I was to invite you, I would be gentle and you would be scared, despite so many, however many years of experience with women, and it would be strange to be scared, and that would scare you, and you would be talking to yourself in your head and telling yourself that it was ridiculous to be scared, of what?

It made no sense, none, and still... you would be scared. I would like it that you were scared, and would not give you comfort. I would have you stand with your hands behind your head and look you over, walk around you, touching gently, maybe speaking quietly to you about what I am touching, the sleeve of your shirt, your hair, your belt, your cheek. You would find it odd and awkward and maybe a little silly, but you would stand there quietly anyway, letting me look and touch and comment.

And maybe you would be prompted to say something into the void to reach out to me: it would slip into the room, fail to seek purchase, drifting awkwardly away when I ignore your words, and slip my fingers under your shirt to touch the skin of your stomach lightly, and maybe you would suck in your breath and close your eyes, and I would tell you to look at me, boy, and you would and I would watch your face while I stroke your skin gently and you would watch me watching as I circle you and trail my fingertips over you.

A touch, an exploration, a claiming.

Water torture

I lay him in the empty bath on his back, cover his face with a damp washcloth, stroking it smooth against his skin.

I hold the cup of water above him, and pour it slowly over the cloth, the sticky terry towelling gaining weight, clinging to the shape of him, his eyes, his nostrils, his mouth.

I see him open his mouth further, like the silent scream, he gurgles, trying to blow the fabric off his mouth as the water slides into it and down to the back of his throat. I watch the material sucking into his mouth as he tries to get air, the steady stream of water unforgiving, his body tensing, his chest rising and falling more quickly, he is making odd sounds, but is not panicking yet. I can see him concentrating on breathing, calming himself, making wet sounds against the washcloth.

The water runs out, he feels a quick reprieve, he draws air in quickly through the wetness, he knows he hasn't much time, his dehumanised body convulsing as if every cell is trying to grab oxygen from the air, his cock hard from fear and anticipation of more. He sucks desperately through the cloth for air.

I refill the cup, I whisper nothing to him, he whimpers before the next stream of water hits the cloth. There are sucking sounds echoing through the room as he swallows water and air, the wetness of the cloth stifling him, and still I let the water run over his face, he squirms and tries not to panic, his faceless body straining against the sides of the bath, the wet desperate sucking sounds are frightening, he tries not to let the fabric gag him, pushing it out with his tongue even as he sucks it in wetly with his breath.

This... this is what it feels like to drown in a cup of water.

Coming home

He buzzes her in, she climbs the stairs and opens the door.

He is waiting there in boxers, kneeling in position, his hands clasped behind his head. He looks up at her expectantly as she enters, doe-eyed and sweet. She tilts his face up to her by his chin, leans down to kiss his mouth, he opens immediately to her, reaching up to stay connected to her lips as she stands. His face breaks out in a broad grin as they separate.

"Hello Ma'am!"

He is all but bouncing, she imagines his tail wagging enthusiastically, it makes her smile.

"Hello beautiful…"

She divests herself of her bag and coat and leads him to the couch, she is tired, it shows. She flops down, he kneels before her and reaches for her boot, undoing the zipper and pulling it gently from her foot, first one, then the other. He strokes her foot and calf through the short stockings she wears, then pulls them off also.

She sighs, rests her feet on his thighs and he kneads them for her. They talk quietly about their respective days, she leans forward, her eyes on his, he reaches for the offered kiss.

She is glad to be home.

Here, boy

We are sitting at the table, chit chat finished.

He gets up, heads to the kitchen to get us drinks. I lean back in my chair, watch him go, wait until he is across the room.

"Come back here."

He turns, his expression a question, a slight frown, concerned that he has forgotten something. He comes back to me.

"Give me a kiss first."

He smiles at me. "Yes, Ma'am!"

He leans down to me, I slip a hand around his neck and pull his mouth against mine, a warm, soft, sweet kiss. I release him and push him gently away. He smirks at me, I laugh and shove him towards the kitchen.

I watch his butt as he walks away, he nearly makes it to the kitchen door.

"Come here."

He pivots on one foot, tilts his head, he does a cute little half smile, walks quickly back to me.

"Yes Ma'am?"

"Kiss."

Another big smile lights up his face, I reach up to

him, he brings his mouth to me, I cup his face and dip my tongue into his mouth, play around his lips a little, he sighs into my mouth. I push him away.

"Off you go, where's my drink?"

He chuckles, almost skips off to the kitchen. He doesn't get there.

"Boy, here."

He turns, he is laughing, he rolls his eyes, exaggerating, he groans as if he is annoyed.

"Yessss, Ma'am?!"

I laugh as he trots across the room back to me.

"Kiss! You never kiss me, geez!"

"Sorry, Ma'am!"

He reaches down for my mouth and I hold him there, soft and tender kisses, nudging at him, he starts to sink under it, he shuffles to get closer to me, I know he wants to drop to his knees. I push him away.

"Off you go then, what... do I have to wait forever for that drink?"

He bounces away from me, looking back every few steps, I let him get around the kitchen door before call him back.

"Here!"

He laughs with delight.

"YES MA'AM!!"

He runs back to me and waits there with a shit-eating grin on his face.

"KISS!" I demand.

We both laugh, still laughing as we lock lips, it is

difficult to stop long enough to properly kiss.

I make him stay there until I get a decent one, until I feel him start to melt.

I shove him away. "Where's my drink?! God!"

This time I wait until I hear him opening cupboards in the kitchen.

Kissing play parties

People go to play parties and hit strangers with implements.

I would rather go to a play party, find some beautiful boy with a stunning, full lipped, 'hurt me' mouth and a shy demeanour, shove him into a corner and just make out like he is the last drink of water in the desert.

To build it up excruciatingly slowly so he doesn't see the violence coming, to make his lips bleed and his eyes run with the ferocity of it and then tenderly make it better with impossible softness and innocent bobbi-sox kisses behind the bleachers before I open him up again. I want to rub myself raw on his mouth.

Is that acceptable play party behaviour?

Face touch

I reach out to your face, you think I am going to pet your cheek, I do that, pet your cheek, or cup your jaw gently or just touch your face, just to touch. I don't pet you though, this time. I cover your face with my hand, it is an odd kind of claiming, you are awkward under it, waiting for... something.

The heel of my hand against your chin, my thumb and pinkie splayed over your cheeks, the other fingertips touching your forehead, your eyes. I can feel your breathing, warm against the palm of my hand, my fingertips move lightly over your skin, a touch to your eyelid, feeling your eye fluttering underneath, moving away to see you peek at me like a child playing.

This melts me, somehow, it is strange and intimate, this covering of your face. I wait for you to try and kiss my palm, but you are still and silent there, patiently watching me, waiting for me to get what I want out of it.

Eventually, I will move my hand to press against your lips, to cover your mouth, to make full contact. I will allow you to kiss my palm, feel your soft lips caress the sensitive skin there, you will close your eyes, and maybe make a sound with the simple pleasure of it. It will make my stomach flip and make me want to press into your face, to feel your skin give, your mouth slightly open as I push against it, your lips moving, and maybe your tongue will slip out and you will lap gently at my slightly salty skin.

And I will try to hold off on pushing harder against you, on grabbing at your face, on tightening my grip, on cutting off your breath... I will try, I will.

And for a while, I will succeed.

Fucking bitch

I knock and wait.

You open the door, your expression at first one of gentle questioning... when you see me your eyes widen, you gasp, like a cartoon character, comical and odd. You almost shake your head to try to clear it. I can see your mind ticking over, a million questions immobilising you...

I smile, savouring your confusion, it is incredibly hot, that vulnerable look. I see you unconsciously opening up, it is immediate and involuntary, as if your skin peels away from your body and falls at your feet, leaving you raw. I see your surrender and it hits me straight to my core, I want to drop to my knees and cry for the impact it has on me, and I know, I know that you feel it even stronger than I do. It is visceral, feral and makes me shake from the inside out and oh my god, oh my god, oh my god... that... that... fuck fuckfuckfuck.

I reach out and grab you with a hand around your throat.

You whimper, your mouth opens, whether to exclaim or to utter some protest I don't know and don't care, I shove you back into the apartment, against the wall, and I take your mouth, violence and teeth, sucking and biting at you like a source of food.

I fuck into you like I want to get to your insides, you make a sobbing sound that breaks me in two, makes me angry.

I feel tears rising.

"Fuck. You! FUCK YOU, fuckyoufuckyou!"

I shove you back into the apartment, back back back until you are against the bed, and I snarl and shove you onto it. I follow you, landing awkwardly on you with a thump, I look at your face and you are crying, your face crumpled and wet, a high pitched sobbing coming from you, your mouth saying words that I can't make out.

We are both crying and I am so so angry with you.

"You fucking little bitch, Fucking. Little. Bitch!!!"

"I know, I'm so sorry, so sorry, so sorry, so sorry Ma'am."

Your voice is a broken sobbing, and I hate you for it.

I kiss you blindly, teeth clashing, your lip bleeds and I suck at it, you writhe under me, your hands held above your head as if you are bound, and you open up for my gnashing teeth, wanting to be hurt, aching for it, reaching for it.

Your openness scares me, you have no resistance, I can feel it. I could kill you now and you would welcome it. You sob into my mouth and it breaks my heart.

I hiss at you, "I missed you so much, I missed you so much, you fucking bitch!"

You make a pathetic sound, look up at me. "I missed you too, I missed you, I missed youmissedyou…"

Your body shakes, you reach up for me, craning your neck to get at me, your eyes wet, you can hardly kiss me back for the crying, and when I slap your face, I feel your relief. I slap you over and over, you hold my gaze between slaps, watching me, willing me on.

"Please, please, please pleaseplease…" You whimper at me and god, you are so beautiful, I want to tear you to pieces.

I tighten my grip on your throat, you close your eyes.

Another strangled "Please…" slips out.

I nod and start to methodically take you apart.

THE FIRST TIME

I put a blindfold on him and stand close.

I lean into his ear, whisper, "You are going to undress me, and kiss me all over, starting at my feet..."

He nods, smiles broadly. "Yes Ma'am!"

He is nervous, eager, shifting from foot to foot.

He reaches out tentatively to make contact with me, starts at the top with my shirt, fumbling awkwardly to get it off, touching my bra when it is exposed, he runs his hands cautiously over the fabric to find the clasp. He does not grope at me, feather touches, finding the clasp, releasing it, easing the bra off my shoulders.

He gets on his knees, touches gently down to my boots, finds the zippers, pulls them off one at a time.

The jeans are next... his face at hip height. He pops the button and pulls down the zipper, peels the jeans off me slowly, like peeling a grape, carefully slipping them down, allowing me to step out of them.

He touches gently at the g-string, I know he wants, really, to stroke the lacy fabric, to run his fingers, mouth, tongue against the sheerness covering my pussy, that he wants to touch and lick and luxuriate in it. To his credit he resists, sliding his fingers into the sides and pulling them down. He waits then, for me to get comfortable.

I lie down on the bed on my back and he starts with my toes. It is delicious, slow and deliberate, soft and gentle. He takes his time, working up my body... toes, feet, shins, knees, thighs, a passing flutter of kisses at my pussy, gentle and teasing, but he doesn't linger there, across my stomach to my breasts, sucking my nipples into his mouth one by one to feel them harden, covering every inch of my skin and on reaching my neck, he nibbles and tickles, then covers my face with soft kisses, he pauses, a slow one at my mouth, to see if I will kiss him back, I don't, his disappointment floats off him... he sits back on his heels and waits.

I roll over, he starts at the nape of my neck, his mouth a soft prayer on my skin, soundless, and wordless, lips and tongue down my back. When he gets to my arse, he lingers. I let him. The kisses turn to gentle licks down the crack of my arse, I raise my hips to him slightly and I hear him moan at the movement, gentle, persistent licking at my hole, soft, then stronger and more insistent, his tongue trying to fuck me, his face pressed into me. I relax into it; hot, sexy, dirty.

I finally tell him to move on, and down he goes, across the backs of my thighs, the crook of my knees, stroking, kissing, licking, down my calves and back to my feet. He pauses when he thinks he is done.

"Am I wet, boy?"

His breath catches.

"Do you want me to feel, Ma'am?"

"Yes."

He takes a deep breath, blindly strokes his fingers up my inner thighs, touches my pussy gently, feeling softness, pushes his fingers between my lips, strokes long and slowly against me, I hear him make a sound as his fingers slip in the silky wetness.

"Yes Ma'am, very," he whispers.

I roll over onto my back again, and direct his face to my cunt. He pauses for a moment, a little off balance, then he licks at me, tentatively, starting with soft kisses, he teases me. It is lovely, perfect, frustrating, I try not to arch up into his mouth, I let him play with me. His tongue glides between my labia and up to my clit, softly and quickly, over and again.

"Slower and harder," I whisper.

He changes pace with my direction, I move his head into position to get what I want. I twitch, move, have him change up, down...

I am not getting there after a while, and stop him. He apologises, he is upset that he hasn't made me come, he plucks at his blindfold, and waits there, murmuring soft apologies. I assure him that it is okay, that I am not done with him yet.

I look around, I need something else, something more...

I get the cane so that I can hit him while he licks me. I draw him back in, wrapping my legs hard around his head, nearly suffocating him. As he licks at my pussy, I randomly hit him with the cane, the sound of his gasp and the shock of the strike reverberating in my cunt each time makes me push up into his face.

I let him go again when it is clear that this is not going to make me come. His blindfolded face looks up at me, forlorn and lost and disappointed with himself. He apologises again, he is upset.

"Please tell me what I can do..." he begs.

I shush him and tell him that if I wanted something different I would say so. There is nothing wrong with what he is doing, I am just... difficult the first time...

I bring him into me again, tell him to stick his tongue out, to keep still and give me his tongue. He does, and I use it as a masturbatory tool. I fuck against his mouth, my clit sliding against the soft wetness of his tongue, he makes little sounds of pleasure as I get more violent against him, shoving my pussy into his mouth.

"Don't you fucking move, bitch," I hiss at him, though I know full well he is not going anywhere.

Finally, I feel that building deep inside, everything stops, there is nothing but me and this reaching to come, it is a desperate singularity, and I fuck against him without coherent thought. I come into his mouth, against his tongue, forever and for a millisecond and forever I am in it, inarticulate with sounds that come from somewhere primal, heart racing, nipples reaching for attention, shoving up into him with all the strength in my hips and thighs. The intensity of it makes my whole body stiffen and shake, pulling his mouth against my cunt with my thighs, until I reach the zenith and then having to shove him back from me, it's too much, the stimulation, and I start to laugh involuntarily at the incredible intensity.

He clings to my hips like a drowning man, seeking contact, cheek pressed against my thigh, arms wrapped around me, laying across me, trying to get closer, he is kissing whatever part of me he can reach, he is worried, can't tell if I am crying or laughing, either is odd... I have not warned him, normally I warn, I did not expect to get to this with him the first time... and still, I am laughing.

I bring him up to me as I come down, heartbeat slowing, breathing returning to normal, I am no longer laughing, I am kissing kissing kissing, tasting myself on him, pulling him impossibly close and closer still, wrapping myself around him until every part of our bodies that can touch is touching and we kiss and kiss and kiss. I am languid then, I remove his blindfold, he blinks into the light, he is wired, jumpy, he is so happy that he has made me come for the first time.

He keeps saying, "Wow!"... "Wow!"...

It is completely and utterly adorable.

He finally gets up from the bed and paces, looking at me, restless, he wants to punch the air, he wants to jump up and down, he wants to shout, it amuses me greatly, and I realise... what he really wants to do... is strut...

A day at work

At work, all vanilla, a normal corporate office environment. A colleague and I are preparing for a meeting.

"Can I go and get a coffee?" he asks me.

I laugh, he really doesn't need my permission.

"No," I say.

He gives me a disappointed look. "Oh... really?"

"No."

His face drops. He looks like a kicked puppy.

"Okay," he says as he gets back to work.

Sometimes work is fun!

Scary movie

We are going to sneak into the movies. His eyes light up, he is delighted and surprised that I want to ("Really?! Really?!!!"). We are naughty children, giggling and running sideways into each other as we sidle into the movie illicitly. A scary movie, my favourite.

We grab a seat and settle in. He knows what I am like with scary movies: I like to be scared, that sudden start of fear, when my everything tenses, that adrenaline rush that makes me grab at him as my entire body jerks. Sometimes I squeal. It makes him laugh, and me too, after the fact.

"A scary movie..." I whisper to him with glee.

He grins and nods as it grows dark.

I reach under the jacket on his lap, my fingers fumbling for the button of his jeans. He does not look at me, he is suddenly shy, embarrassed. He blushes as his cock (my cock) hardens under my insistent groping. He shifts down in his seat to give me better access. I lean over him, my mouth against his cheek, he turns to find my lips with his and I open my mouth to him, welcome the taste of him.

I hold the zipper taut as I undo it slowly, hot breathless kisses, he makes a soft sound into my mouth as my hand squirrels its way into his boxers. I pass by his cock, one stroke over it causes him to lift his hips to my touch. I wrap my fingers around his balls, he spreads his knees wider for me. I roll them between my fingers, getting into a comfortable position. I am finally content, and hold him, cupping his balls gently in my hand.

I pull my mouth away from him and whisper into his ear, "You know what happens when I get scared, don't you?"

He pauses for a moment, thinking, picturing it...

When I get a fright everything tenses, I grab at him painfully in my fear, normally his hand, his thigh, his arm, but this time... I watch him figure it out. When I get scared, I am going to hurt him, badly, my fist will close involuntarily around his balls, hard and sudden and jerky, without control.

He nods slowly, solemnly. "Yes, Ma'am."

I smile happily at him, twitch my fingers against him, settle back and wait for the movie to start.

Blow job

She crawls backwards, down his body, skin sliding on skin as she slips against him.

He is restrained, open, vulnerable beneath her. His chest rises and falls quickly, deeply, almost hyperventilating as he waits, cock hard in fear and anticipation of what comes next.

She looks up at him, an amused expression on her face, her mouth close to the head of his cock, she does not touch it, breathes against him, watches it pulse as if it is a living creature, as if it would reach for her. He does not move.

The corner of her mouth curls upwards as she parts her lips, snakes her tongue out between them, touches the tip wetly to him. He is sensitive now, she hears a sound, a sucking of breath, or sharp exhalation, she isn't sure.

A quick dip of her head and she takes him into the warm soft surrounds of her mouth, fast, sudden, she slides her lips down his cock abruptly, strongly, her tongue lubricating the way, then backup just as rapidly, one stroke, she almost hears the 'pop' as her lips release his cock back into the air. A desperate groan from somewhere above her, quick breaths, she sees a twitch in his thigh muscles as he forces himself to keep still. He does not move.

She licks her lips, moves into a comfortable position. She stares at his face for a moment, he is beautiful, mouth open, eyes focussed on her, he sinks into her gaze, expectant and lost, she wants to kiss him again and always, to swallow that look that he gives her. He parts his lips a little further, his tongue peeks out to touch them, oh god... he is teasing her. She swears inwardly, her stomach lurching with that aching need, he pretends to be oblivious, she loves that. And still, he does not move.

She leans down, laps once at the tip of his cock, a long leisurely stroke around and over it, he hisses, his whole body tensing. She flushes at his reaction, heat rising, she takes the head of his cock into her mouth and closes her teeth on it, no lips, just... her teeth... gripping his cock in her mouth, firmly... with her teeth.

She smiles to herself, and then, she waits.

It takes him a moment to realise that there is nothing happening, that she is not moving, that the pressure of her teeth on his flesh is not abating, that she is just... waiting. The moment seems to stretch out, she feels saliva gathering in her mouth, and lets it drip out onto his cock, she wonders vaguely if he can feel it.

"Would feel nice," she thinks.

She knows he is puzzling over what to do, a million thoughts whizzing through his mind...

Tickticktick at the speed of light.

She gives him no help, she just... waits. And then, he moves.

He tenses his arse beneath her and tentatively raises his hips, pushing his cock up into her mouth, slowly, her teeth scraping against the sensitive skin of the underside and top. Perhaps he thinks she will relent and relax the pressure, she doesn't, of course.

He makes a whimpering noise as he pushes his cock into her mouth against her teeth, she hears the slight sound of it through her jaw, the rasping. He groans as he continues the push and then withdraws, slowly, an edge of desperation in it. And again, he presses his hard cock into her mouth, her teeth bared, scouring his sensitive flesh, the pressure consistent and painful, he carries on.

This blow job with her teeth continues, agonisingly slowly, he makes a keening sound, like a wounded animal as her teeth abrade his skin over and over. She stays still, just varies the pressure a little, clamping down tighter when he seems too comfortable, easing her bite when she thinks he can take no more. She drools all over his cock, unable to swallow properly, and still, she feels his skin catch and skitter across her sharp teeth, the wetness doesn't ease the scouring.

And when she thinks he is close to giving up, she slides her lips softly against the length of him; respite, deep and long, her tongue slipping against the aching skin, and then, back to teeth.

He scrapes himself raw on her, relentlessly hurting himself, hard and desperate, whimpering and gasping for breath as he drives himself in slow motion against the pain.

Order my lunch

He worries about me from over there, across the ocean... I eat badly and don't sleep... He expresses it gently, quietly, persistently...*(worry worry)*... It is sweet, this concerned caring.

I tell him, then, to order me a salad online for my lunch, something that allows him to contribute to looking after me, to extend that concern in a practical way. The salad bar is downstairs from my work. The choices are endless and relentlessly healthy: fresh greens, spinach, snow peas, carrots, artichokes, baby corns, green beans, tomatoes, olives, jalapenos, chicken, tuna, different dressings. I tell him he can add whatever he wants to the salad (no anchovies!). He puts a lot of thought into it, I can see his mind ticking over.

"What will she like?"

"Is this a good combination?"

"Which dressing?"

He has a level of fretting and concern that it will not taste good, that I will not like it, that he will get it wrong. He orders, tells me it is done, and waits for me to come back to him...approval, or no.

I go downstairs at noon like a good girl to pick up

the healthy lunch he has put together for me. It makes me laugh softly to myself, it is hot and sweet and a mash up of the dynamic, which I love.

And it is a treat, a tasty surprise (oh, chilli... and egg!), he has done well. I feel holy and healthy and sweetly cared for as I crunch through the vegetables that I know I should eat more of.

I think to myself, "This will make him happy," as if I am some submissive girl, pleasing her master. That thought, too, makes me laugh as I make a mental note to tell him 'No jalapenos next time'.

I look forward to making him do that again.

Thinking about...

This morning I was thinking about you in Florence.

Only this time the guy pulled a knife while he was sucking your cock because he knew you were going to bail, and he told you to push his head onto your cock, and you did. You pulled his mouth onto your cock, shoving the length of it down the back of his throat, lost in how good it feels, terrified and hard, with him holding the knife against your groin.

He stopped before you came, removed his mouth from you, and stood up, and with the knife at your neck made you kiss him, properly, and you were scared, with his pulling your mouth against his, his urgent insistence. The taste of your cock between you, his tongue raping your mouth.

And you were thinking about what else he was going to make you do, looking to the door, wondering if you would make it if you bolted for it.

Then snippets: him shoving you onto his bed and ripping your pants down.

"Show me your arse, boy."

And then it was me and not him and you are trembling and you roll onto your stomach and with your face down on the bed, you get up on your knees with your arse to me, and I run the knife in a line down the crease of your butt, over your hole, pushing against your skin until I think it is going to cut you. Then I press a little harder and I cut you, moving down to your balls, and raking the knife over them at random and then against the underside of your cock. There is blood.

And you are making a moaning sound and shaking and I hit your cock and balls with the flat of the knife and that makes your body rock, and I am him again, and I am looking at your arse, my cock hard and heavy, and I rub it against you, whatever part of you I can reach, sliding it between your cheeks then down, between your legs, slipping against the blood.

I roll you over and shove your legs up and hold the knife against your cock, the tip pressed tight into the flesh, and I shove my cock into your arse in one brutal thrust, and you try to get away because it fucking hurts and you have your eyes squeezed shut, and your mouth open and I fuck you, dry and wretched, feeling your arse tight around my cock, so fucking tight and I slap your face and tell you, "Look at me, you fucking bitch!", and I shove my cock harder into you and look at your face and I call you a 'prick tease' and 'a fucking idiot foreign tourist'. I tell you that you are no more than a fuck-hole and I am going to bring my friends around to teach you a lesson, and I am slapping your face and you can't look at me, and I keep telling you, "Fucking look at me while I fuck your arse!", and my fucking you is pushing you up on the bed and I keep having to pull you back down, slamming you onto my cock.

And I shove my fingers into your open mouth and you can't help it, you suck on them, and that makes me laugh because you fucking love this, you slut, and I shove as many fingers as I can into your mouth, fuck your mouth and throat with them, your body convulsing as you gag and that hits my cock, and I tell you, "Fuck me!" and you want to do what you are told.

"Fuck me, you fucking little whore!"

And I stay still and you are grabbing onto the bedclothes, trying to get some leverage to shove yourself against my cock, and my fingers in the back of your throat are doubling up your body, which makes your arse push against my cock, makes you squeeze it, and I like that so I shove my hand as hard as I can into your throat, saliva running out of your mouth, and it hurts your mouth and throat and I am concentrating on your fists, grabbing desperately at the bed trying to get a grip to shove yourself against my cock, desperate to fuck my cock like you are told, and I think about closing my fingers around your throat and then I come.

Kissing, is all

I saw a boy today that I wanted to kiss.

On my way to work on the train, he was maybe 40, fit, a little rough, with a strong imperfect face, unconventionally beautiful and serious, wide jaw, furrowed brow, a shock of thick dark messy hair. I stared at him. Sunglasses on, I watched him. His face came alive as he talked to a little girl, became sweet, gentle, soft smiles. He had much-regretted tattoos, mostly hidden under his sweatshirt, occasionally he looked my way, once locking on, not really with interest, mild curiosity. I didn't look away, staring rudely, not sure if he could tell behind my sunnies that I was simply watching him. He blinked first, bowing his head, a small puzzled smile curling the corner of his mouth.

He leaned back, ran his hand through his hair, and I felt a familiar, much-missed lurch in the pit of my stomach, not strong, not compelling, but oh so welcome and I nurtured it, drifting.

I wondered what he would look like with an expression of shocked surprise on his face at having his hair gripped in a tight fist and his head jerked back. I imagined his mouth in an 'oh' shape, that delicious 'oh' that says 'ow' and 'please' and 'fuck' and 'oh my god' all in one. That 'oh' that invites contact and violence and tenderness, that 'oh' that says he is suddenly a little unsure, *that* 'oh'... that one.

I wondered what his face would look like on the edge of coming, that moment when he reaches for it, that serious, yearning, desperate expression, that moment when he thinks it's inevitable, then the one immediately after when he realises it's not.

Mostly, though, I wondered what his mouth would look like, softening at the approach of a kiss, how his expression would change, reaching hopefully for it, anticipating it, waiting for it. I wondered what he would taste like in those early, soft, exploratory kisses and thought, with him, that he would taste slightly unclean, rough musk and saltiness, of dirt and sweat.

I wondered how he would react to those mouth-touches, the ones where I barely brush his lips with mine. The ones where I tease the bottom edge of his top lip with the tip of my tongue, lick and suck gently. I pictured his confusion, slight awkwardness in that position, mouth slightly open, waiting, accepting, as I slip inside just enough to taste that silky inner moistness that feels already intimate, invasive, like sex, insistent but barely there.

I wondered if he would be still while I lap at him like a kitten, all gentle and unhurried and breathy, and how he would react when I push him back from me when he reaches for more. I wondered about the kisses where I nudge at him with my mouth, encouraging him to open up to me expectantly, watching his desire grow, wanting depth and hunger and aching for that moment when it turns from this gentle play into something else, but giving him nothing more. The ones where I promise with mock aggression and don't deliver, while I wait for his gentle acceptance to turn into a frustrated and desperate desire for attack, watching for the change, wanting to restrain, ride and match it all at once.

I watched him until he left the train at the stop before mine, my mind full of his mouth, his face forgotten already, less important than the slow rise of hunger for kissing.

BEG ME TO BE ALLOWED TO COME

"I'm going to untie you," she told him, idly stroking his cock.

"Yes Ma'am," he replied, breathing heavily, his cock hard and leaking pre-come from all of the activity so far, his nipples aching, his arse tensing to stop him thrusting up into her hand... he's dying to come.

"Are you listening?" she demanded.

"Yes Ma'am." He nodded and looked up at her, his eyes clouded with need.

She leaned down to whisper into his ear.

"I'm going to untie you and bring your mouth to my cunt – you are going to lick me until I come."

He felt goosebumps, butterflies in his stomach, his cock jumping. He nodded quickly.

"Yes Ma'am."

He wanted to smile, but daren't, he wanted this so badly, he didn't want to blow it.

"When I come, if I come," she added pointedly, "you are immediately going to shove your cock in my cunt and fuck me... do you understand?"

He nodded again, stifling a moan that was rising in his throat at the thought.

"Yes Ma'am."

"Repeat it back to me."

He stammered, afraid of failing already, distracted by her fingers playing with his cock.

"Uhhmm... you are going to untie me...and I am going to lick you until you come," he looked at her, a question in his eyes, saying the words making his cock leap. She did not respond, so he continued. "When you come, immediately after you come, you want me to... errm... you want my cock in your... uhhmm... cunt... and... ermmm... you want me to fuck you... Ma'am?"

He waited for her approval, holding his breath, his mind temporarily off his cock, which she was still stroking softly with her fingertips.

She smiled at him. "It sounds even better when you say it."

He smiled broadly back, his breath escaping in a hiss, relieved. "I have to disagree there Ma'am... when you say it, it's much hotter."

She laughed. "One more thing..."

He waited, his heart beating a little faster, wondering if there was some cruel twist.

"You will not come when you fuck me... Do you understand?"

He nodded wildly again, his mouth already salivating in anticipation of tasting her, he would have agreed to anything.

"Yes Ma'am."

She reached over him and undid his bonds. She lay

beside him, gripped his hair to guide his head down her body, his tongue already out of his mouth, flicking out to touch any part of her that he could reach on the way down to her pussy.

She held his mouth at her cunt and shoved her hips up toward him as she pushed his head down.

His mouth, tongue and nose smashed into her wet pussy and she felt him trying to lick her, but he could barely move as she fucked his face; his nose and mouth full of the smell and taste of her. She writhed against his face, keeping him still against her, she closed her thighs on the sides of his head and felt him desperately trying to lick her as he had been instructed, but his mouth was so tight against her he could hardly breathe, much less lick. She fucked his face for what seemed like ages, he tried to pull away so that he could breathe, but she held him hard against her, feeling him trying to gasp for air. Finally she relaxed her grip and pulled his wet face away from her cunt. He took deep panting breaths, her musky wetness all over his face, he looked up at her.

She tightened her grip on his hair, guiding his face back to her pussy, gently this time, and he started to use his tongue on her. He licked her with the flat of his tongue, lapping at her lips and towards her clit, gentle, then flicking softly at her clit on the upstroke. He did this over and over until the flicking started to elicit a thrust of her hips towards his tongue, and she started holding his mouth up towards her clit.

He played around her clit, teasing her, touching it only glancingly, and she moved her hips to chase his tongue, but she did not guide his mouth elsewhere, it was perfect, teasing, delicious. She moaned and tightened her grip in his hair when his tongue slid over her clit. He wrapped his arms around her thighs, stroking her hips, her belly, as his mouth moved on her. His fingertips travelled her skin, stroking her in time with his licking. She heard him groan into her pussy. God, she wanted to smash her cunt into his fucking face, to hurt him with it, but the soft licking was what made her come, so fucking frustrating, so fucking good.

He started to lick at her clit with the tip of his tongue, she moved her hips against him to guide the pace, he sucked her clit hard into his mouth, she felt a flash of pain and gasped. She closed her fist hard around a handful of his hair, ripping at it, jerking his mouth away from her harshly. She reached down and slapped him. His face flew to one side, he looked up at her, his face pained.

"Too much," she hissed.

He blushed, stricken. "Sorry Ma'am! Sorry sorrysorry…"

She brought his mouth back to her clit and he cautiously licked at it, moving his tongue against her, softly, then harder, then softly again, finding a rhythm that matched her hips thrusting against him. His efforts started to draw reward as she began to moan, her thrusts against his tongue becoming stronger, her fingers convulsively gripping and releasing his hair. She wanted more, more contact, more of him.

"Two fingers, inside me," she demanded.

He immediately slipped two fingers into her wetness, fucking her with them in time with his tongue against her clit, she felt the pressure of his fingers against her and pushed back into him. He licked her forever, changing pace, rhythm, and the force of his licking, his tongue starting to tire, his jaw to ache, pacing himself to the movement of her hips against him.

Finally, she started to make inarticulate noises, her moans becoming guttural sounds, compulsive sounds. He felt her start to tense, and he increased the rhythm and force against her just a little. She started to utter low little cries that made his cock twitch and he groaned against her cunt.

He felt more than heard the sound coming from deep in her throat, she gripped his hair, pulling at it, holding him right there as she came, convulsing, every muscle tensed, her hips lifting off the bed, her grip taking him with her, her thighs tight against his face, keeping his mouth against her as a sound escaped her in a long guttural groan. She came hard for several seconds, holding his mouth on her, finally and suddenly pulling his head away from her, his tongue licking at the air as she pushed his mouth away from her.

She moaned softly in the aftermath, her body relaxed, eyes closed, and she pulled his head up towards her face by his hair.

He quickly slid up her body, his knees pushing her legs further apart, her grip bringing his wet mouth to hers as his cock found her pussy. Her mouth was already on his when he entered her, moaning, she felt his hands slide under her arse to lift her to him. She kissed him, hungry, tasting herself on him, pulling his mouth to her, sucking him into her. She lifted her hips to take him deeper, she knew he could not last long.

She was sucking the breath from his body, her mouth voracious on his, her nails digging into his back. He panted into her mouth as he fucked her, hard, long strokes, a sound coming from deep in his throat, he felt as if he was going to explode already. She reached between their bodies, gripped both of his nipples and pinched hard, he grunted in pain, his face contorting as she twisted and pulled at them. The pain made his hips slam harder against her and she lifted up to him with each thrust.

It wasn't long before he pulled his mouth away from hers.

"Oh god, I'm going to come... Ma'am," he groaned.
"STOP!! Don't you fucking dare!"

She stopped moving under him, gripped the hair on the back of his head hard with both hands, pulling his face harshly away from her. He tried to look down at her but couldn't from the angle at which she held him, his face twisted in pain from her pulling his hair, his hips still, his cock throbbing inside her.

"Don't you fucking dare, boy," she repeated.

He was breathing heavily, obviously concentrating hard, his eyes shut, lips compressed. She waited until his breathing started to slow a little.

"Are you under control?" she asked.

"Yes Ma'am."

She released her grip on him and started to rock her hips against him again, her legs going around his arse, her hand going between their bodies so she could feel his cock sliding into her cunt. She pulled his face to hers, kissing him softly. He groaned, and met her thrusts with force, pushing her fingers harder against her clit.

She grunted softly and felt him respond, his hips slamming into her, his pace increasing, his breath quickening. She arched up to him and shoved her mouth against his, teeth clashing as she reached for more of him, she whispered, "Yes, yesyesyes yes," compulsively into his mouth.

He drew away from her again, breathing heavily.

"Unnghh... Please... Ma'am, I'm going to come... Please!"

"NO!" she commanded. She stopped moving.

She felt him fight the urge to slam his cock into her and come inside her, he was making soft grunting noises, his face a picture of concentration, his mouth open, panting, his muscles tensed. She waited.

As his breathing slowed, and he started to relax a

little, she stroked his face and he looked down at her.

"Beg me, beg me to be allowed to come in my cunt."

He didn't hesitate. "Oh god, please Ma'am, please please please please Ma'am, please let me come."

"In my cunt, say it."

"Please let me come in your... cunt... Ma'am, please please please," he begged, his face flushed. His mouth looked desperate, she wanted it badly, his mouth.

"Boy..."

"Yes Ma'am, please Ma'am, please let me come in your cunt, please Ma'am..."

"You may come... When you do, you will look at me, do you understand? I want your eyes on mine when you come."

He nodded madly. "Yes Ma'am, yes yes, thank you, thankyou."

She shifted under him, her cunt and arse tensing to push up against his cock. He needed no more encouragement and he circled his hips, taking it more slowly, wanting to draw it out now that he knew he would be allowed to come. He closed his eyes, pulling his cock almost all the way out of her, and dipping just the head in and out.

She smiled and fucked up suddenly hard against him, driving his cock deep into her. His face registered the shock of pleasure and he realised he was not going to last as she fucked up against him again.

He gave in to her and slammed his cock into her

hard, groaning. She pulled his mouth down to hers and fucked his mouth with hers as her cunt drove up against him.

She moved his head to one side with a grip in his hair and closed her teeth on the flesh of his exposed neck. She dragged her teeth over his jugular, biting down on his skin, moving suddenly to that spot that she knew drove him wild, grinding his skin between her teeth, sucking his flesh into her mouth and pulling at it. The shock of pain drove him over the edge, he felt himself start to come and he moaned in surrender.

She felt him starting to lose it, she gripped his hair tightly with both hands, making him wince. She held his face close to hers, locked her dark eyes on his, watching his face contort as if in pain, his body tensed, his hips pushed hard against her and she gripped him tightly with her legs, pushing up to him, he kept his eyes on hers as he came. Their eyes locked, his mouth open, he thrust hard into her, a continuous grunting sound coming from his throat, the moment of raw openness was almost enough to make her come again.

And as he finally relaxed his body into hers, gasping for air, muttering words that didn't make sense, she wrapped her legs around him and stroked his face, pulling him to her, kissing his softening lips, nudging his breath from his mouth, whispering "Good boy, good boy..." as he melted into her.

Dressing up

The couch, the television, the vanilla boy, I'm bored.

"I want to dress you up."

He looks over at me, then looks back at the television.

"Come on, it will be fun, we can put a dress on you... no, my skirt, the black mini. You will look sweet. And that cute top with the flowers..."

"Ssshhh... I'm trying to watch this."

"... and stockings, my thigh highs... not sure my shoes will fit you though... maybe. And make up..." I touch his lips. "... lipstick, eye shadow, mascara for those beautiful lashes... you will be gorgeous..."

"Errmm... how about... no."

I sidle up closer to him and touch his thigh, leaning into his ear.

"...no? But really, it will be great fun, we can be girlfriends, it'll be sweet... you will look beautiful..."

"Look, I really don't want to, okay?"

"I will help you get undressed first..." I whisper in his ear as if I haven't heard, and I touch him, undoing buttons and zippers as I talk about each article of clothing. "...your shirt first... then your jeans..."

He shifts a little at my fingertips on his fly.

"... your boxers...", and he eases his arse up off the couch towards me a little as I touch him. "... then when you are naked, I will dress you again... it will be fun, I promise..."

"No! Look, I'm trying to watch this..."

"... I'm thinking really red lipstick, that would be great, and that plum coloured eye shadow... your eyelashes are going to look amazing with mascara on..."

"Oh for fuck's sake!"

He jumps to his feet and storms off towards the bedroom.

I watch him leave and sigh.

The couch, the television, I'm bored. The programme finishes; another one starts. Bored.

I hear him come back into the lounge room and turn towards the sound with a scowl. I look at him and he blushes and does a kind of shuffle.

He is wearing my highest heels, awkwardly, they are too small, and his legs are encased in black stockings, his blond hairs sticking out here and there. My black mini sits well on him, he is lean in the hips, I am stunned that it fits so well. He has on a pink shirt, stretched tight tight across his chest, unable to do up all the buttons, I see a black bra underneath. His lips are red red red, and slightly smeared, his cheeks pink (with eye shadow, I think), his eyelids have some colour I can't quite make out, and his lashes, even from here, are luscious and thick with mascara.

I smile at him and he looks so shy and embarrassed I could throw him to the floor and fuck him right there. I go to him and put my arm around his waist and kiss him chastely on the cheek. My voice drops a tone and I feel a little silly as I put on a bit of gruffness.

"C'mon in sweetie, I'm glad you could come over."

He picks up my tone immediately. "Errrmmm, thanks for inviting me over," he replies primly and allows himself to be led to the couch.

"You look beautiful," I tell him as he sits down awkwardly, the skirt riding up his thighs.

I openly ogle his legs and he self consciously pulls the skirt down a little and looks at me accusingly. I stroke his stocking encased thigh and lean into him, my mouth at his ear.

"Your legs look very sexy," I tell him, my hand sliding up under the skirt feeling stocking turn into skin.

He pushes my hand away, again gives me another accusing look and turns his face to the television.

I press in closer to him and try another tack, my fingers touching the buttons of his blouse, stroking his chest, playing at the top of his bra.

"I love this shirt," I tell him. "But really, showing your bra like that is a little slutty."

My fingers slide into his shirt and under the cup of the bra to find his nipple. He slaps my hand away.

"Stop that!... Please!"

I am starting to get turned on with this game he is playing with me because I can see how it will go and I already feel the aggression rising.

I turn his face to me by his chin, 'What did you come here for if not for this?" I ask and shove my hand up his skirt.

He forcibly pushes my hand away, and tries to slide away from me.

"I came to watch TV with you, that's all!" he shrieks.

"I don't think so," I reply.

I lean into him and I kiss him.

His mouth answers me even as he tries to back away, and I grab his hair and hold his head still as I take his mouth. When I pull away, his lipstick is smeared all over his mouth. I wipe my mouth with the back of my hand.

"You come here dressed like a slut, what did you expect?" I hiss at him.

"You said I looked beautiful," he says plaintively, convincingly.

"No, you look like a slut, look at you in that tiny skirt and your buttons half undone and too much makeup!" I snarl. "You want this!"

His eyes widen. "No!" he manages before my hands are all over him.

I'm undoing his shirt buttons and grabbing at his bra, lifting it up to get to his nipples, pinching them, and I straddle his lap in that tiny skirt and I can feel his hard on through it which is both obscene and sexy and I pull at his nipples and bite his neck and he is still protesting and ineffectually trying to stop me.

"Stop, please stop, I don't want this!"

"Yes you do, you slutty bitch, I know you do!"

I slide back in his lap a bit so I can get my hand up his skirt and feel where the stockings stop and his skin begin, I feel lace and his cock sticking out of my panties and knowing he put my panties on is somehow incredibly hot and I try to shove the skirt up to his waist so I can get at him and he lifts his arse off the couch to let me.

I pause and look down at him under me and he is incredibly hot. His mouth smeared with lipstick, his eyes framed dark with mascara, his shirt half off, his bra pulled up to reveal his nipples, his skirt bunched around his waist, his lace panties pushed aside, his cock straining for attention.

I grab both his wrists and hold them behind his head, leaning into him, rubbing against his cock.

"Didn't I tell you this would be fun?" I ask him.

He looks up at me and nods.

"Tell me you're a slut," I whisper in his ear. "Tell me you want this and I will give it to you."

And he does, and I do.

Pimping him out

See this boy here... 6', dark hair, expressive mouth, pretty eyes, clean shaven... he's articulate, intelligent, slightly bruised but still usable...

(lift your shirt, boy)

... yes, yes, you can see that bit of damage there, but it doesn't impact his performance... he's available to you... you want him?

(turn around, boy)

... well for anything really, doesn't matter... no, it's not up to him... yes, well a gag and some restraints will take care of that, so don't worry...

(open your mouth a little)

... yes, see that, oh yes very soft, pliable, yes see how I can just slide my fingers in, you see how his eyes close, very sensitive to that...

(suck them, boy)

... if he's been good, he does like a bit of a beating, also being forced, he quite enjoys that... yes, that's okay, you can touch him, tell me how you want him...

(bend over that table, boy)

nod Yes, yes it is lovely isn't it, run your hand over it, like this... did you feel him quiver, delicious isn't it?... yes, quite reactive, works if you are gentle or rough... you want me to show you, of course, I'd be happy to...

(come here, boy, so I can...)

laugh Did you like that? Oh yes, he makes some beautiful sounds when you do that, and, well, you can see how he responds, yes he's quite lovely in that state isn't he... oh, anything really... groups... well again, once he's restrained it's all a bit out of his control isn't it?

No kissing though, I reserve that, no not under any circumstances... yes, I would appreciate a report after the fact, I like to know that he is performing well... I will inspect him for damage after you are done, bruises are acceptable, but anything more will be extra...

You want?

Body canvas

He is restrained on the bed, he is spent, his skin glistening with sweat, his chest rising and falling quickly, his mouth open as he tries to catch his breath. I have left him for a moment and he opens his eyes to scan the room for me. He finds me at the foot of the bed, gazing at him as prey, still hungry. I climb onto the bed between his spread ankles. He lifts his head to watch me and I show him what I have in my hand. He stifles a smile when he sees a ballpoint pen, and I feel his tensing body relax.

I move forward and slide up his body, skin against skin, until my mouth is at his ear, my weight languid and heavy against the length of him. I lie there for a moment, reaching up, interlacing my fingers with his. I shift against him, fitting my curves into his angles, breathing into his ear, savouring the heat of him under me. His slowing breath gently raises and lowers my body against him. I want to melt into him through his skin.

I touch my lips to his ear.

"Who do you belong to baby?" I whisper.

I feel him crane his neck to caress my cheek with his, hear a stifled moan deep in his throat, though he has no more want left in him. I press my cheek against him, soft, he slides his lips against my face to my ear.

"I belong to you Ma'am," he whispers back.

I nod against his cheek.

I sit back on him, my knees on either side of his body, and uncap the pen. I wipe his chest with the sheet, he studies my face, amused. I catch his eye and my mouth curls in a half smile, he smiles back, broad, open, trusting, and my heart skips a beat. I touch the tip of the pen to his skin and trace the first letter of my name on him, long and flowing and gentle. I follow the same path of the letter again, the pen is fine-point, and sharp.

I press a little harder the third time, then harder again the fourth. The fifth time, he winces, by the tenth, he is gritting his teeth and shaking his head, by the thirteenth, I am using some force and he tenses, squeezing his eyes shut, hoping the skin doesn't break.

By the fifteenth, his whole body stiffens as his muscles contract against his restraints and a whimper escapes his lips, the pen like a knife, following the letter's path.

I shift against him, rocking just a little, hunger rising. I move onto the second letter.

When I have finished, some considerable time later, his skin is covered with my name, repeated over and over, the black ink surrounded by raised angry redness, his body an aching declarative canvas.

I lean down to his ear.

"Who do you belong to baby?" I whisper.

"I belong to you Ma'am," he whispers back and I nod against his cheek.

Ask me to hurt you

She calls him to be with her at 6pm sharp. In the meantime, she prepares, already walking through the scene in her mind. Feeling herself moisten in anticipation. She puts the ankle and wrist cuffs by the door for him. She readies a bottle of champagne, tempted to have a glass, but wants her senses alert.

Then she waits.

She hears the door open and turns towards the sound. He comes in, as usual, knowing what to do, and undresses quickly, looking at the ground, sneaking glances at her as he puts on the cuffs, already semi-hard . She looks at her boy with satisfaction when he kneels before her in perfect position. She grabs his hair in her fist and pulls him hard towards the bedroom without a word. He stumbles awkwardly on his knees, but she keeps her grip, and forces him forward. She stops in the doorway, tilts her chin at him and pulls him upward, pulling him to his feet. She attaches his wrist and ankle cuffs to the four eyebolts in the door frame, his body stretched.

Then she pours a glass of champagne, and approaches him. She touches him lightly, with her fingers, her cold champagne glass, back, shoulders, nipples, stomach, he shivers. She holds the champagne glass in front of his mouth, the beaded condensation wet on the outside.

"Lick it," she whispers.

She watches closely as his tongue laps at the glass, and she laps at his tongue in turn, hissing softly if he so much as turns his head towards her to get more of her mouth.

She sits down in the armchair in front of him in the bedroom, her legs crossed, swinging her boot gently from side to side, sipping her champagne. She watches him, he looks unsure, uncomfortable, goose bumps rising on his skin. Finally she smiles at him. He smiles back, nervously anticipating what is coming.

He makes an irresistible target; her fingers itch with the desire to hurt him.

She puts down her champagne and approaches him. She smacks his cock lightly.

"Down boy, down," she says and laughs softly when it has no effect.

She brings the handle of the flogger to his lips.

"Kiss it," she whispers again, and watches his mouth closely as he does.

"Lick it," she says, and as he does, she again laps at his tongue with hers, breathing into his mouth, giddy with his soft lips and the wetness of his licking tongue.

She steps back and stalks around him, touching every part of his body, stroking his back again, his arse, his balls, his cock, his stomach, his nipples. She stops at his nipples to give each a sharp pinch, watching his face as he registers the pain and gasps.

She moves close to him, bringing her mouth to his, he strains to reach her, but she stays just out of range. She grabs his hair in her fist, holding his head still and delivers feather kisses to his mouth. Then she quickly pushes forward, pulls his face into hers and takes his mouth hard, bruising his lips, aggressively raping his mouth with her tongue, pulling his mouth into her and pressing her body hard against him. She hears him moan into her mouth and feels her heart skip a beat, her pussy throb.

She reaches down between them and pulls hard on his pubic hair and hears his sharp intake of breath. She feels his muscles as he tries to push himself against her hand, but the restraints stop him from moving. She leans back, still gripping his hair, pulling it painfully, and looks into his eyes, and melts a little as she sees his willingness to give her what she needs, his face screwing up at the pain.

"Ask me to hurt you, tell me how much you want it," she says softly.

"Please hurt me Ma'am, I want it badly, please, please hurt me, I need you to hurt me, please, please..."

She nods and lets go of his hair and hears his hiss of relief. She moves around behind him, he is looking over his shoulder at her and she smiles at him.

Then she starts.

Softly at first, just enough force to swing the strands in a line against his back, and he thinks for a moment that it will be bearable. He always thinks that.

She builds up slowly, alternating strikes against his back and his arse. She gets into a rhythm, back-back-back-arse, and she watches him relax into it, calm, as the strikes hit him like a metronome, his back and arse turning red. He starts to grunt softly at the strikes.

She interrupts the rhythm, steps into him. He reaches for her with his mouth, his whole body straining against the cuffs. She presses herself against him, rubbing her cheek against his, straddling his leg to press her pussy against him, her breasts against his chest. Her hands go around to his warmed back and arse, and she scratches her nails down the tender flesh as she brings her mouth to his.

His response is immediate and violent, crashing his mouth against hers with a moan, sucking at her breath, his tongue finding hers, his entire body trembling to get more contact with her. She digs her fingers into his flesh and kisses him back, hard, pulling his head towards her to smash against him, teeth clashing, his lip catching and he winces, but doesn't pull away. She finally steps away from him, and his eyes don't leave hers until she is out of sight behind him again.

She really goes to work on his back and arse now, swinging hard, enjoying the sound as the strands hit him. She watches his muscles as he starts to really feel it, and tries to flinch away from the blows, but there is nowhere to go. She checks in with him regularly and his reaching for her becomes more gentle, less urgent, dreamy as he loses himself in the pain, so she steps in to kiss him, nudging his mouth open, touching him, bringing him back to her, whispering "You can take some more for me, can't you boy?" to which he always answers the same, "Yes Ma'am."

She raises it up a notch, now putting force into the blows, his body rocking with it. He no longer flinches, but keeps his body open to her. He starts to make a continuous sound that starts with something inarticulate and ends up being her name repeated over and over through his laboured breaths.

"Tell me with every blow that you love it," she whispers to bring him back to her.

By now he is whimpering, his mind drifting, his body a sheet of pain, and his voice cracks as he tries to do her bidding.

"Ugh, I love it... Ughhh...I..loveit..."

She knows he is struggling to stay with her, and his voice deteriorates into grunts that are edging into panic as he tries to find a place to put the pain he is taking for her.

She finally starts to slow down and she feels his relief and disappointment when she stops.

She steps back to look at her handiwork and strokes his damaged skin. She leans into him from behind, pressing herself into his heated body, her hands wandering over his chest, abs, hips, pulling him back against her, her mouth at his ear, she says, "Good boy," and hears a sob escape his lips.

The chair

You are naked, I am clothed.

You're sitting in a chair, looking up at me, waiting, anticipating. You are not restrained this time. I smile at you, and drink in your return half smile. A questioning look on your face, but you know better than to ask.

I pull my skirt slowly up my thighs, your smile widens as you watch. I see you twitch, your cock already getting hard. I approach you and straddle your legs, my skirt raised so that I can feel your thighs against mine, skin on skin. My weight is fully on you as I slide forward, your cock touches my panties and I press against it, leaning into you. I'm already wet.

Your arms go around me, sudden, tight, pulling me hard against you, your hands going to my arse to pull my pussy harder against your cock, pressing up against me, reaching up for my mouth, taking my breath.

I lean back and slap your face, hard. Your eyes flash, hurt, defiant, I can feel that you want to ignore it but you daren't.

I lean to your ear and whisper, "You can touch what I say, when I say."

You nod, chastened. "Yes Ma'am."

"Put your arms around me, gently."

You nod again. "Yes Ma'am."

I feel your hands on my back, snaking around my body, under my shirt, your fingers touching as much as you dare, around to the sides of my breasts, down to the top of my arse, up to my shoulders.

I rub a little against your cock, take your face in my hands and bring your mouth to me. You let out a soft moan and squirm a little. I stroke your lips with my lips, the tip of my tongue wetting them just a little. I breathe into your mouth, wanting so badly just to have it, to own it, to eat it. I start to kiss you, soft, feather kisses, gently sucking your lower lip into my mouth, touching it with my tongue.

I whisper into your mouth, "Buttons," and feel your hands at my blouse, obediently undoing buttons.

I kiss you, and I melt into your mouth and I taste your tongue and it goes on forever and I'm so fucking wet and I rock my wet panties against your cock.

"Breasts." I whisper.

Your hands are immediately there, pulling my bra out of the way, rough, grabbing, pinching my nipples and I bite you and smash my mouth against yours, I feel teeth clash and wince.

You're struggling to get more contact on your cock, and I'm sucking your breath and I can't get enough of your mouth. I'm trying to breathe and I'm panting into your mouth and tasting your tongue and wanting to get inside you and I can't get enough of your mouth.

"Pussy," I growl.

One of your hands goes between our bodies and I shift to give you access. I feel your fingers against me, you hold me away from you, touching me gently, stroking the crotch of my panties softly, frustrating, delicious, perfect. So fucking frustrating.

I can feel you smile against my mouth as I try and push my cunt against your fingers. I want to slap you, but I can't bear to let go of your mouth, and it feels like the chair is going to tip as I try and fuck against your fingers.

I finally groan and release the kiss to slap your face full force, and again, and again.

I hiss into your ear, "Stop fucking around and make me come."

Your fingers push aside my panties and find my clit. I fuck against your fingers feeling the wetness all over your hand, sliding against your cock as I thrust against you. I want more of your mouth, but I can't breathe, so I rest my lips against yours, leaning into you for support, ragged breaths, hard and fast, concentrating on your fingers against me, inside me, all my muscles relaxing and tensing against you.

When I come, I come hard, arching back, inarticulate cries, every muscle tensed, my nails digging into your skin, trembling, your fingers sliding inside me as I grab your hair in my fist, pull your mouth onto mine and gift you my orgasm.

When I get like this

When I get like this... when I get like this, I can't breathe. My whole body is wired, hyper-aware and it feels like I am huge, like I am bursting out of my skin, like the body that contains me isn't big enough to hold this feeling, will explode with it, like my skin will split and I will not slowly bleed out of it as much as burst out in a new guise.

And you are here, right HERE, and I am looming, which is the word, the right word, 'looming', huge and dark. And you are afraid, even though you know it's me.

I crawl, which might seem odd for a dominant woman, but I do. You are here, before me, you are kneeling, always. And I crawl towards you, relentless, and I am so fucking ravenous, I want all of you and I don't know which part of you I want most, or first, or next, I want it all and I want it all now and I am not big enough for that and I don't have enough mouths, hands, cunts, to take you all at once. But I want you, all at once. And when I reach you, I keep crawling, straight over you, like some huge machine that will suck you up as I cover your body with mine.

And I start with my mouth low, at your cock and

you want me to sucklicktonguekissbite, but I am only there on the path to absorbing you, and my mouth is all over you, all parts of you, all at once as I move up your body and I push and I push and you are forced backwards, and it is awkward and you try to stop yourself tipping and I am still moving forward and as I move up you are forced backwards, I can feel your body under me, your skin hot and sweating and I keep crawling over your body and as my mouth reaches your mouth, you are bent backwards and I am all over you, your skin burning under me and I am like a huge gaping maw and you are disappearing into me, my cunt taking your cock inside, my mouth swallowing yours, and it's not nearly enough, and all of me is aching and prickly and every touch hurts and you are hard and melting and when I stop and put my weight on you, you start to tremble with the awkward position I have forced you into and I don't care and I put my weight on you and you moan and I cover you, all of me swallowing all of you and it's still not enough, and I get into your head and I consume your thoughts, your emotions, your feelings and I take them all into me and they become mine and when I am finished all of you belongs to me.

I want you. I fucking want you.

PEGS

She told him to get up on the bed on his knees, and he scrambled up, kneeling on the edge, his hands cuffed behind him. She took out the three pegs he had brought with him, the 'macho 'pegs, the marquee pegs, the 'hold-things-in-a-cyclone' pegs and smiled at him. She brought her mouth to his left nipple, sucking and biting at it before putting the first peg on him, she took quite a bit of flesh, her mouth having made it slippery. She repeated this with his right nipple, and stood back a little to look at him.

"Does it hurt?" she asked him.

He looked relieved. "No, not a lot," he admitted.

She stroked him from his neck to his navel, then moved the pegs to just be on the tips of his nipples and saw him wince, his eyes squeezing shut, his face screwing up with pain. He had never had this done to him before, and he shook his head violently from side to side, mouth and eyes squeezed shut.

"You can swear if you want to," she told him, watching his contorted face closely, thinking it looked beautiful.

"Fuck... fuck... fucking bastard...FUCK, FUCK...!!"

She laughed softly, and wondered, really, if he did

this for her, this swearing, because he knew she loved it. She didn't think the pegs hurt that much, but the sound of him in pain made her stomach turn over with lust.

She chased his mouth, even as the swear words poured out, but he was shaking his head from side to side, trying to find somewhere to put the pain.

She held his head still by his chin and caught his mouth, she kissed him hard and he kissed her back, his mouth opening to hers, her violence in the kiss making the pain lessen.

She kept asking him if it hurt, and he kept saying, "Yes, yes, YES!"

His answer getting shorter and more frustrated. He was wincing, struggling, not paying attention to her due to the pain. She trailed her fingers over him. His boxers were wet with pre-come, his cock hard.

She told him he could ask her to take the pegs off if he wanted. He didn't hesitate.

"Please Ma'am, please take them off."

She kissed him again, waiting until she had his attention from the pain, until he put himself into the kiss. When he started to melt into her, she grabbed both pegs and released them. He gasped, the pain momentarily spiking. As it subsided, his body slumped in relief, his face relaxed. She moved close to him, watching his face.

"Do you want to see how wet this makes me?" she asked, looking into his eyes.

He risked a smile.

"Yes Ma'am," he nodded, his face open to her now, his pain forgotten.

She undid her belt and jeans slowly. He leaned away from her a little so that he could watch as she slid her hand down into her panties. She was very wet and her fingers slid easily down her pussy. She stroked herself, amazed at how wet she was. She brought a glistening finger up to show him, then put it on his lips.

"Do you want to taste me?" she asked.

His eyes were on hers, his mouth already open, his breathing shallow.

"Yes please Ma'am."

She slid her fingers into his mouth. He licked at them, his tongue slipping over and between them. She thrust her fingers in and out of his mouth gently, feeling his tongue lapping at them as he sucked at her taste. She pulled them out and wiped them lightly against his boxers, feeling his cock leap under her fingers.

"Do you want to feel how wet you make me?"

He licked his lips. "Yes, please Ma'am."

She considered making him beg, but she felt as if he was struggling a little with all this newness, that it was all he could do to stay with her.

She leaned into him, reaching behind him, pressing against his skin, and undid his cuffs. She brought his left hand out from behind his back, took off the cuff and guided his hand down her flat stomach into her panties.

He was fumbling a little, and she covered his hand with hers and pushed it down. He made a noise in the back of his throat as he found the wetness and slid his fingers along her pussy, his mouth open, his breathing heavy. She pushed his hand down so that his fingertips just entered her, then pulled him up slowly, feeling his fingers wanting to get more of her, wanting to find her clit. She rocked against him just a little. He brought his other hand to her hip to pull her to him.

She shoved it back behind his back and hissed, "No!"

She pulled his hand out of her pants and directed it to his mouth, he licked his lips and he waited, looking into her eyes. She wondered if he was going to beg, but he waited, his tongue already moving in anticipation. She shoved his fingers hard into his mouth, and he sucked on them, his eyes never leaving hers.

"Was I wet?" she asked unnecessarily, pulling his fingers from his mouth.

He nodded and smiled at her.

"Oh yes Ma'am."

She smirked at him, nodded slightly.

She covered his eyes with a blindfold, placing it tenderly, stroking the silky fabric. Unable to resist his mouth, she held his hands behind his back, and pressed against him for a kiss. She played with the fact that he couldn't see, pulling away and coming back to him suddenly, watching his mouth anticipate the contact, then denying him. Watching his hunger grow.

Finally, she stepped back from him.

"Undress me," she instructed him.

He reached blindly for her.

Thinking

Thinking...

About masturbating.

Thinking about you, and thinking about masturbating.

Thinking about you, spread-eagled, restrained and blindfolded.

Face up, on a bed.

And I touch you, with my fingers, my mouth, my hair, my breasts.

Different places, all over, in different ways, to see how you react.

And if I get what I want I do more of it.

Like I might expect if I licked your cock from base to head with the flat of my tongue.

Or if I nipped the inside of your thigh with my teeth.

Or if I stroked your lips with my breast and then a nipple.

Or if I licked and nibbled at your neck, right at the jugular.

Or if I straddled your chest and rocked my cunt against you, wet.

Or if I held your head still by your hair and kissed

your mouth without letting you kiss me back.

Or if I rubbed your cock softly with my pussy, just stroking it in the wetness.

Would you fuck up against me to get more contact?

I would move out of your reach, because I would love to see you fuck up towards me and not get what you want.

And maybe if you looked like you wanted it badly enough, and you moaned in frustration, I would take your mouth with mine and swallow the moan down my throat.

And maybe I would bring my cunt up close to your mouth.

And maybe I would ask you how much you wanted it.

And maybe I would stroke myself, close to your face.

And linger on my clit, and it would make me moan.

And maybe I would slide two fingers inside myself and back up to my clit, and down again in a hypnotic motion.

And bring my fingers to your mouth, and touch your lips.

And keep my fingers touching your lips, wet, so you can smell me, and make you beg to taste me.

And if you begged, I would slide my fingers into your mouth and gently fuck your mouth with them.

Sliding them over your tongue and whispering, "Lick me baby."

And maybe your tongue would feel so fucking good that I have to have it on my cunt.

And I would lean down and kiss you, with my fingers still in your mouth, and my tongue in your mouth, and ask you if you want to lick my cunt.

And maybe I would straddle your face and bring your mouth up to me, and watch your tongue reach for my cunt and keep it just out of reach.

And hold your head away from me by your hair and ask you what you are waiting for

And feel you pull against my fist in your hair.

And maybe if you said please enough times, I would relent and bring your mouth to my cunt and let you lick me.

And I would want to fuck your mouth, but I would want the licking more.

I would want you to make me come, but maybe, maybe you wouldn't be allowed to.

So maybe I would stop you if I was close to coming.

And I would tell you that you don't get to make me come.

So maybe I would kiss you, taste myself on you and whisper that maybe next time.

Excruciating isn't it?

Delicious.

I'm so fucking wet.

Like an itchy, restless, wellspring of want.

Tears

I have you in cuffs, face up on the bed, but only your ankles are restrained. You have one hand stroking your cock, the other is covering your face. You are making a muffled sound through your fingers. I realise you are trying not to cry. I make you remove your hand from your face and I look at you. Your mouth is trembling, your face contorted. My pussy throbs, and I stroke your face.

"Let it go baby."

A heartbreaking sob comes out of your mouth and I want to fucking eat your mouth. Your body is wracked with sobs, you convulse with the strength of it, and I am wet. I can hardly breathe I'm so turned on and I cover your lips with mine and rape your sobbing mouth with my tongue.

And you can't kiss me back, you are crying so hard, and tears are escaping the corners of your eyes and running down your face. And I want them on my cunt, those tears. I'm ravenous for the weeping and the tears and the hurt and whatever it is that is making you like this.

I don't know why you are like this and I don't care.

I straddle your chest, feeling it heave under me, and I lean forward to feel it against my pussy. And you are still hard and you are still stroking your cock and you are sobbing your heart out, mouth open, eyes running.

I move up to cover your mouth with my pussy, and you sob and you lick me and I feel your tears on my thighs and your body is shaking and still you lick me and I don't have to look to know that you are still hard, and your crying resonates in my cunt and I move against your mouth relentlessly and it's one of the hottest things I have ever felt.

I know you

I see you heading home. I already know where you live: I have been watching you. I follow you.

You are distracted as you turn into your building and I follow you up to your apartment.

My pulse quickens as I watch you open your door. I catch up, step quickly in behind you and close the door.

You turn and look at me... A tall blonde has followed you into your apartment and your mind can't quite grasp what that means.

I look you up and down: You are wearing khakis, desert boots, a blue button down shirt, a cap. Clothes familiar to me. You wear that uniform a lot as you go about your day. I give you a half smile and you cock your head, a quizzical look on your face. I am wet already.

I step towards you and you take a step back, there in the entrance-way of your apartment. You look over my shoulder at the closed door, and I can tell you are looking for a way to get me out. I take two more steps towards you with a smile, you step back. Your back is to the wall.

"Hey..."

You are genuinely puzzled, but not yet frightened.

"Shut up!" I retort quickly.

You start to laugh, a nervous laugh, until you see the expression on my face, which makes you stop.

"I said shut the fuck up!"

I show you the knife in my hand: small, evil-sharp and still your look is confused, you don't understand what is going on. I grab your throat and shove your head back and it hits the wall with a thud. I apply some pressure and watch your eyes widen and I want to fuck you so bad, I can taste it. With the knife at your neck, I bring handcuffs out of my bag.

"Hands behind your back, boy," I hiss, and I quickly fasten them before you can get your bearings.

I pull you from the wall and shove you into your apartment. I can see that you are still not getting it. Maybe you think I am here to rob you, who knows what you think, who cares. I knock your cap off your head and rip your shirt open, buttons flying. You are looking at me and I see the lights go on.

"What the fuck...??!"

"Didn't I tell you to shut the fuck up?"

I slap your face and see the shock register. I slap you again, and again, full strength, your face flying from the force of it. I streak my nails down your chest, hard, leaving trails of red. And again and again I tear at your skin. You are flinching, stepping back away from me until your knees hit the couch and you can either sit or stand. You choose to stand; your eyes are racing around the apartment, looking for something, some way to get me out of there, to distract me.

"You make a sound and I will fucking cut you," I hiss, the knife still in my hand, poking at your ribs.

I undo your belt, the button of your pants and take down your zipper. I laugh when I see you are hard.

"You fucking slut, you want this, I knew you would."

You start to protest. "No, I fucking don't, you crazy bitch!"

You sound angry, but you are blushing, embarrassed, hard.

I shove your pants down, along with your boxers, and your cock is rock hard, leaking pre-come. I smack it, once, twice. You wince and cry out and I grab your pubic hair and pull it hard and lean in to snarl into your face.

"Didn't I tell you to shut the fuck up?"

I grab you by the neck and shove you around behind the couch. With your pants around your knees, you nearly fall over. I push you over the back of it, forcing your face down into the cushions, your ass up, inviting me. I want to fuck you so bad.

I start to hit your ass, smacking it hard, over and over, finding a rhythm, watching it redden, and your hips start to move with my smacking, and I realise you are rubbing yourself against the couch, and it makes me fucking crazy.

"Are you getting off on this, you fucking slut? I haven't even started with you yet!"

I shove your shirt up to expose your back and again I scratch you, from your shoulders to your hips, feeling your skin come off under my nails, red streaks left behind, your back arches under my fingers and you start to make little mewling sounds as I hit the same spots over and over.

"Don't fucking move," I whisper. I press the knife into your ribs for emphasis.

I quickly take my t-shirt off, my belt, jeans, panties. You don't move, waiting there, your back and ass now reddened, blood seeping from the deep scratches, your breathing heavy.

"Please, please, please, please please," you keep repeating compulsively. I have no idea what you are pleading for, but nothing is up to you anyway.

I can feel my own wetness at the crotch of the panties in my hand. I lean over you, and god, the contact of your hot skin makes me ravenous. I press against you, my thighs against yours, my pussy against your ass, my breasts on your back, your cuffed hands between our bodies. I pull your head back and shove my panties into your mouth.

I rip your belt out of your trousers and move quickly to the front of the couch and attach it to the couch leg in front of you. You watch me as I am doing that, my panties in your mouth, your wide eyes scanning my naked body, but they keep flicking back to look at the knife in my hand and you shake your head. I quickly undo one of your cuffs, loop the chain through the belt, and relock it around your wrist.

I look into your wide eyes.

"I'm going to fuck your ass, you fucking slut, and it's going to hurt. You're going to like that aren't you?"

You shake your head violently at me and I see real fear for the first time. I slap your face.

"You're going to like me fucking your ass, aren't you?" I ask again.

You shake your head again, your eyes pleading with me.

I slap your face again; you are still shaking your head. I slap you over and again until you stop shaking your head and your eyes are filled with tears, from the pain of the slapping or from the acknowledgment you have to make I don't know.

"I said, you are going to like it, aren't you, you fucking slut?"

You nod, slowly. I want to fuck you so bad.

I move back to your ass, I have the strap-on in my bag. I step into the harness quickly, tightening the straps around my hip. The large silicon cock slips easily against my crotch. I look down at my cock; hard, veiny, pulsating in my hand.

"It's not so very big,' I say to you as I run my fingers over your ass.

You flinch away from me, which makes me want to

shove this cock into you in one hard thrust and listen to you scream against my panties in your mouth. I gather some wetness from my pussy and I play my wet fingers around your asshole, wanting to laugh as you lift your ass towards my touch as I rub against you, and you start again, grinding your cock against the couch as I play my fingers around your ass.

I shove a finger, two fingers into your ass, no longer playing, no longer gentle, and you cry out into your gag. You pull away from me, but there is nowhere for you to go and I fuck you with them. I press against you as I move them in and out of your ass, my thighs against yours, my cock resting on your ass. When you start to push back against me, I lean down to your ear.

"You greedy fucking whore, you love this don't you?"

You moan, I think you are shaking your head again. I want to fuck you so bad.

I place the head of my cock against your asshole, I slide against you a little, I apply a little pressure, feeling the push of it on my clit and I wait.

"Fuck me," I demand.

You make a sound into my panties. I smack your ass, already red, over and over.

"Fuck me, boy," I say again.

You push back against me and it's so fucking sexy it makes me growl deep in my throat and I hold my position, watching my cock press against your ass. You are moving against me, and I thrust hard into your ass, and the head of my cock pops in and you make a high pitched sound. I wait there, circling my hips against you, but not pushing any further, teasing myself with the pressure on my clit.

I lean forward over you, grab your shoulder and thrust into you in one hard movement. You scream into the gag as my cock brutally stretches your hole. I lie forward against you, my hips against your, my breasts pressing into your back, my cock inside you, all that skin on skin.

Then I start to fuck you, moving so that the strap-on hits my clit over and over, and I grab onto your hips to hold you right there in the spot where I can just circle my clit against the pressure. Rubbing, adjusting the position, involuntary moans escaping my lips. And when I stop, I feel you shoving back against me even though your sounds of pain are continuous.

"I knew you would love this, you dirty fucking slut," I gloat.

It feels like I am fucking you forever and the force makes your cock rub against the couch and you make muffled grunting sounds through the gag and they feed my hunger. You push back against me, fucking me and I wonder if that bucking against me and that groaning meant you had come, but I don't care, I just want that pressure, that rubbing and finally, with the thrusting and the fucking, I come in your ass, hard, shoving my cock into you with as much force as I can muster, I prolong the pressure against my clit, and it's so fucking good, the strength of it shaking my body against you. I finally collapse against your back, catching my breath.

I undo the straps, leaving my cock in your ass as I step back.

You are making some strange wet snuffling noises as I quickly dress, minus the panties. I move around to the front of the couch and kneel down in front of your face. You look up at me, your eyes wet with tears, your nose running, my panties still in your mouth.

"You loved that didn't you, you fucking cock-slut?"

Your face shows resignation as you nod your head wearily. I rip my panties out of your mouth.

"Tell me," I demand.

You lick your dry lips with your dry tongue and your eyes can't meet mine.

"I loved it," you whisper.

I hold your chin up. "Look at me, you fucking slut and tell me again, say it."

You look into my eyes, your lips moving without a sound and I wait. You flush a bright red and you let out a sob.

"I loved it, you fucking my ass, I loved it," you whisper, barely audible.

I nod. "I know you," I say.

I throw the key to the handcuffs down on the couch and I walk out, leaving the door open behind me.

Welcome home

She sighed as she walked through the front door, throwing her briefcase by the hall table. She smoothed her skirt, shrugged in her jacket, took a deep breath and turned to look into the lounge room.

He was sprawled on the couch in jeans and t-shirt, comfortable, had been watching television. He had glanced up when she entered and now he was looking at her, a half smile on his face, a question in his eyes. He knew better than to approach her without permission when she got home from work, so he waited.

She caught his eye, and held his gaze for several minutes, assessing her mood. Making up her mind, she called him. "Here, now."

He beamed at her and her heart skipped a beat. He leapt off the couch and did a running slide to her across the hardwood floor, ending up on his knees at her feet. She laughed, leaning down to bring his chin up to her and kissed his mouth softly.

He immediately reached up for more of her kiss, his lips aggressively opening hers, his tongue in her mouth, tasting her. She felt his hands reaching for her, and before she could stop him, they were on her breasts, his fingers seeking out her nipples.

She pushed him backwards away from her. Her eyes flashed.

"Greedy slut," she hissed.

She could see his hardening cock outlined against the front of his jeans, she grabbed a fistful of his hair. Her heart was racing, a combination of lust and steely disapproval making her head spin.

She leaned down and whispered, "What exactly was that?"

He breathed his apology into her ear. "Sorry, sorry Ma'am... I missed you!"

She leaned away from him, holding his eyes with hers, keeping him still by his hair. She drank in the uncertainty in his eyes before she slapped his face, watching his eyes register the sting and the shock that always appeared, even when he saw it coming. She didn't need to look to know it made his cock strain harder against his jeans. She took a deep breath, holding back a sound rising in her throat. She slapped him again, and god, his expression... she swore to herself that if she just kept doing it, this one thing, she would come just from watching him react. She slapped him again, he let out a soft moan.

She leaned down and rubbed her cheek gently against his warm reddening face, and imagined she could feel the sting against her skin.

She stalked into the lounge room, knowing he would follow. He crawled as quickly as he could after her. She flopped down on the couch and held her foot out to him. He kissed her black boot and let his lips brush her ankle before pulling it from her foot. She sighed with relief and offered her other foot where he repeated the ritual. He knelt back and waited for further instructions as she regarded him.

"Strip."

He quickly pulled his t-shirt off over his head. His pants were more difficult given he was kneeling, but he had done this many times and was quickly nude, kneeling, waiting.

She lifted one foot up to his shoulder, her skirt riding up her thighs. He stared directly and unashamedly at her crotch, his mouth slightly open, breathing deeply to take in her scent as she widened her legs. She applied pressure with her foot to the side of his face, and he followed the pressure sideways until his cheek was against the floor, her foot holding his head down.

"On your back," she whispered.

He rolled over onto his back, and she rubbed her foot from his face, down his body, stroking his cock with it, applying pressure to his balls, then sliding it back up to his face. She stopped with her foot over his mouth.

"Lick it."

He reached out his tongue and she felt him lapping at the arch of her foot. He held her ankle gently with both hands and brought every inch of her foot to his mouth, straining to reach her toes to suck them, to taste her. When she was satisfied, she offered her other foot for his attention. She relaxed back against the couch, letting the day go.

She finally took her foot from his mouth, stood up, hiked up her skirt and straddled him, whumping down onto his chest so his breath left his body in a huff, her bare arse in her g-string against his chest. He drew gasping breaths as she pulled his arms down, and trapped them against his body with her knees and legs on either side of him. She shimmied up towards his face and pulled his head up by his hair so that he was facing her crotch.

"Is this what you want, boy?" she asked as she widened her legs and inched a little closer to his face.

His eyes on her, he tried to nod.

"Yes, Ma'am, please, please."

He strained to get to her with his mouth, but she was well out of reach.

"Well what are you waiting for?" she questioned, disingenuously, knowing he couldn't reach her, watching him crane his neck, trying regardless.

"You want to taste me, boy?"

"Please Ma'am, yes, please, please let me taste you, I'm begging you please let me lick you, please..."

While he watched from inches away, she brought her fingers to her crotch and scratched gently at the fabric covering her pussy, pushing the material against her wetness. She slipped her fingers inside her panties, and slid them along the slickness, from her clit, where she lingered for long enough to feel her muscles tense involuntarily, down to slide easily into her, making her fingers wet.

She drew her fingers out of her panties and offered them to his mouth, knowing he could smell her, watching his tongue desperately trying to reach her fingers.

"Do you want it, to taste me?" she asked him again.

He moaned in desperation.

"Please Ma'am, please yes yes please let me taste you."

She put her wet, slick fingers on his lips and slid them into his mouth. He sucked on them greedily, moaning as he tasted her. She fucked his mouth gently with her fingers, his tongue licking madly at them, trying to get it all. She leaned forward to watch him closely as she fucked his mouth a little harder, sliding her fingers over his tongue, further into his mouth. He opened his mouth wider to accommodate her and sucked hard at her fingers, his low moans hitting her like a sledgehammer.

Her fingers slid into the back of his throat, surely all her juices gone now, but still he sucked on them greedily. They hit the back of his throat and she felt his throat close as he gagged, and his body convulsed. She forced her fingers back there again, his gag reflex more sensitive now, and he choked and gagged, trying to get away from her fingers. She slid them in and out again, shallower, fucking his mouth, feeling his tongue on them, then shoved back deep into his throat again, closely watching his face go red, tears welling in his eyes as he gagged. She kept her fingers deep in his throat, giving him no relief as he tried to pull away, gagging, struggling, choking. His tears running freely down the sides of his face made her pussy throb.

She pulled her fingers out of his mouth and he struggled to catch his breath. She shimmied down his body a little so that she could lean down and kiss him softly, nudging his lips open with hers, letting her tongue taste his violated mouth as he tried to catch his breath. She licked his tears, salty on his skin, and the tenderness she felt almost broke her heart.

Standing suddenly, she turned and walked towards the bedroom, shedding her clothes as she went. Jacket, shirt, bra dropped to the floor, knowing he would pick them up as he followed her. She undid her skirt and stepped out of it, leaving it on the floor also.

She didn't look behind her, but could picture him crawling quickly after her, picking up her clothes, watching her retreating arse. She waited there in the bedroom for him to reach her.

Undressing

While waiting for the lift, she kissed him softly, drawing his face to hers with her fingers in his hair. A first kiss, exploratory, tasting him a little.

She kissed him a little harder once they were in the lift, experimenting a little with her mouth on his, leaning into him, holding his mouth to her by his hair. He was suddenly shy, nervous, she could feel it in his hesitation, his breathing quick and shallow.

When the lift doors opened, she led him to her room by the hand, she opened the door and he walked in ahead of her and stood there, waiting expectantly. She shut the door behind her, and went to him, standing so close she knew he felt stifled, invading his space, her face inches from his, she was taller than his six foot in her stilettoed boots.

She gripped his hair again and kissed him more aggressively, biting at his lips, licking his tongue. She held his head back from her mouth by his hair... he didn't reach for her, but waited passively for her to continue. She looked into his eyes, trying to read him, finding it difficult. She kissed him both softly and hard, and he returned the kisses tentatively. She expected he was terrified of doing the wrong thing. She pressed against him while kissing him aggressively, she felt his cock rising against her, his breath catching when she released his mouth.

She started to touch his skin under his shirt, stroking him. She nudged against his neck, then closed her teeth on his skin and he flinched. She quietly reminded him about his safe words and made him repeat them back to her.

She gestured for him to raise his arms, and she slid his shirt off over his head, and walked around him, touching his bare skin gently: his chest, his nipples, his stomach, his back, his arms. She undid his jeans and slid her fingers down his pants. He stood silent, still, his breathing shallow, his eyes closed as she touched him. She told him to open his eyes, to look at her. He complied and she studied his face. She tried to read his expression.

"Are you doing okay baby?"

He looked into her eyes and nodded. "Yes Ma'am."

She sat on the bed.

"Take your jeans off."

She watched him strip. He left his boxers on, charcoal, as ordered. She told him to lock his hands behind his head and explained that this was the 'Stand' position. She then had him 'Stand wide', with his feet apart. He complied quickly, a questioning look on his face until she nodded approval and she saw his relief in the acknowledgement.

The position made him stand proud and straight,

his abs stretched, his arms flexed, his cock hard, pre-come marking the front of his boxers.

She loved seeing him like this.

She looked him up and down, slowly, drinking him in. He was fit, lean, strong, his eyes showed a mixture of fear and doubt, his cock revealed his desire, his breathing still shallow and quick. He hated silences, and she knew her staring unnerved him, and still she stared silently at him. He looked so nervous, she tried not to smile.

"Kneel," she said, finally.

He dropped to his knees, his eyes downcast. She watched him. He had never knelt before, he looked uncomfortable and her heart melted just a little

"Come here."

He moved awkwardly towards her on his knees. He stopped about a metre away from her and looked up for approval. She beckoned him closer. He shuffled forward but still not close enough so she beckoned him again, widening her legs so he had room to come right up against the bed between them. He looked up at her.

She took his left wrist and put the heavy leather cuff on it, enjoying how it looked. She did the same on his right wrist and told him how pretty they looked.

"Don't they look pretty?" she asked him.

He agreed. "Yes Ma'am."

She laughed, and called him a liar. "You don't think they look pretty at all, do you?"

He smiled, relaxing just a little.

"No Ma'am, not really."

She reached behind him, leaning against his chest to connect the cuffs behind his back. He had never been cuffed before, had never been restrained before. Her face was close to his, and she felt him tilt his head to rub his cheek against hers. She let him get that comfort from her as she attached the clips and she waited there for a moment to let him get used to how it felt.

She sat back up and he looked up at her, he was open, looked a little like a deer in the headlights. She held his face in her hands and kissed him again, opening his mouth, demanding, feeling hunger rise now that he was more helpless, pressing her crotch into him, pushing against him, her legs on either side of his body, wanting to feel his skin through her jeans, the heat of him. She felt him trying to rise to her, the first time he had truly responded to her as she wanted and she felt an ache in her throat. She finally let his mouth go, her lips felt bruised, her breathing heavy.

She told him to get up on the bed on his knees, and he scrambled up. She took out the clothes pegs he had brought with him at her request and smiled at him.

AGGRESSION

Aggression, teeth grinding jaw clenching aggression, barely contained muscle tightening growling aggression. And I need it to go somewhere and I need it to be released and I need a target and I need to come.

I need to fuck and I need to fuck with and I want him invisible and irrelevant and I want him empty, a receptacle, with no eyes and no name. And I want him to be hard, all over, I want lean muscles straining, biceps and a six pack and hard thighs, a cock that weeps pre-come and a mouth that screams and begs and skin that reddens and welts and bleeds sweat on a body that fights against bondage without hope.

And I want that hopelessness and I want to hurt him everywhere and watch the panic and I want him gasping for breath and I want tears and kisses that bite and I want to hit him with everything I've got and make him beg for more and I want to tear apart his muscles and watch them melt and I need to come.

Art and movies

She leads the way into the gallery, their fingers entwined, she takes a look around: black and white photos on the walls, men in pain, women in bondage, lots of men on men, all dark, broody, lots of flesh and leather. She nods towards what will be their starting point and lets him lead the way there. He stops in front of the large photograph and she steps in behind him. She leans into his back, her face averted from the photograph in front of them, her mouth at his neck. She relaxes into him.

"Describe it to me," she whispers into his ear.

And he does, he starts talking softly in honeyed tones, describing the dirty, base, obscene photograph in his beautiful voice, and she feels his voice enter her like liquid, the vibrations of it humming into her chest and she breathes against his neck, his words making her draw the image in her mind, a sharp exhale against his skin when his description hits her pussy, hearing his voice catch as he registers her response. He keeps the monologue going, he finishes describing the photograph, but he doesn't stop speaking to her.

He is no longer describing the photo, he starts describing things he knows she loves. Hot, sexy things that he knows make her wet. She makes a soft sound and he knows he has it right as she presses against him harder, and he leans back into her. He keeps talking to her and her hands reach around his body, pulling him back, her lips now on his neck, and she holds him firm against her and he feels her hips push against him.

And he keeps talking, drawing depraved pictures with his words, and she holds his hips still, and tight against her as she almost imperceptibly starts to fuck against his arse, making a soft sound through her lips against his neck. She tenses and relaxes against him, hardly moving, her breasts rubbing against his back, her hips and crotch trying to get more contact against his arse.

Finally he runs out of words, his breathing heavy, and they stand there in silence, and they feel the heat of their bodies hard up against each other, and when she can almost breathe, she whispers, "Fuck," breathlessly in his ear and he hears her smile and he nods.

"I know."

And they move onto the next photograph.

Movie

When they get to the short film festival, the nature of the films is clear from the crowd milling about in leather and latex outside.

They don't wait but head straight in, finding seats towards the back.

It is already dark.

They hunker down and her hand finds his knee and slides up his jean-clad thigh, coming to rest at his crotch, against his cock. She wants to feel what in the films makes him hard, to understand what goes on in his mind.

She feels him shift, and starts to smile as his cock hardens under her touch. She waits, and his cock presses insistently against her fingers. She laughs and turns to him.

"Stop it," she says.

She knows he is blushing, there in the dark, but he laughs also.

"I can't help it," he says.

She can see his teeth flashing at her, there in the dark.

And his laugh makes her want him, and she reaches for him, pulling his face to hers and she kisses him, and he is still laughing, and she kisses his laughter, her hand still on his cock.

When she pulls away, she looks at him again through the darkness.

"Now seriously, stop it," she says, and waits to see what he is going to do about it.

Hurting

I woke this morning thinking of you, restless. In my head I felt like an animal pacing a cage, restless. Couldn't breathe, coming up from sleep with this violence in my mind.

I want you at my feet and I want to hurt you. I don't have a focus, just hurt, I want you on the floor, whimpering.

The thought of you being there made me so fucking wet, I was breathing heavily with the image of it. Cruelly pinching your nipples until your eyes tear up, fist in your hair forcing your head to the ground, making you lick things, the ground, my feet, I don't care, it's the licking. My foot on your face, too much pressure, you squirming, not wanting to move away, knowing I need you there, and still the licking.

Grabbing your hair in my fist, hard, pulling, awkward, your neck twisted, lifting your face to me. Shoving my fingers into your mouth, feeling soft, wet, holding your head still, making you gag, watching you struggle to breathe, eyes tearing.

Slapping your face, watching your eyes even as they register alarm and hurt, and again. Nipples again, I know you love that, but I want it to hurt badly, like they are going to come right off your body, or you wish they would. I want you to moan with pain and struggle not to twist away, and I know you would do that for me.

I don't want to use things, I want to hurt you with my hands, my mouth. Biting you, hard, leaving marks, blood, licking it. Pinching soft flesh as hard as I can, the inside of your arms, your inner thighs, your balls, your cock.

I want tears and inarticulate helpless noises and whimpering and melting and an edge of panic and hurt in your eyes. I'm incredibly aroused with wanting this, to hurt you.

Come here and beg me to hurt you.

Because I can

I was punching him over and over again: his face alternatively screwed up with pain, mouth open in a silent yell, then stoic against the hurt, completely closing down, trying to get control back. His body thrashed violently against the restraints at the peak of each wave until I could no longer aim the strike and had to stop.

He was so fucking pretty when he was like this: not thinking, just reacting. Some fear, a hint of betrayal, a tilted-head smile when I would talk to him between the punches.

I put on my mock sympathy face "Awww... does it hurt, baby? But you are *invincible*..."

It was a word he had thrown at me earlier.

"INVINCIBLE!" he had declared. Funny.

More punching, that same spot... over and again. His body almost throwing me off the bed with the violence of his reaction, despite his restraints. Powerful, hot... so fucking hot.

I manoeuvred myself so that my pussy was within reach of his fingers. It was awkward, his wrist cuffed, tied to the corner of the bed. I pulled his fingertips against me, and watched his face change as he felt how wet I was, how wet he made me. His entire body relaxed, his face blissing out a little as I shoved my cunt against his hand.

"THIS is why we are doing this... THIS is why..." I said.

He nodded, a tiny smile playing at his mouth. He made a soft sound as I fucked against him, his fingers slipping inside me easily. Maybe a minute or two before I got back on top of him.

"Why do you like it?" he asked. "Is it the pain or the reactions?"

"...because... I like *you*..."

"Yes but you can have me without the punching..."

"Because I can. Because you are so beautiful..."

I had no better answer.

I looked at him lying there, waiting. I readied my fist, watched his brow furrow. He took a deep breath. I let my fist fly.

Romance

I enjoy you so much.

I like it when you tell me what is going on in your head in the moment when we are playing: that you want to come, that you want to fuck me, that you are feeling/ thinking/ wanting things. I love watching your face, and feeling how your body moves. I love your cock and that spot that always wants attention. I adore your mouth, for kissing of course, but also for how it moves, how your lips tense with concentration, how you grimace with pain, how your aggression shows there, how your mouth opens to reach for me, how it softens, lips swollen, all receptive and soft and inviting.

I like also when you tell me things afterwards, and I always forget to ask you about it, to talk about it. Like when you tell me 'it's nowhere near as much pain as I can take' and 'I like how you hurt me' and how you manoeuvre for more which I find hot and sweet and hot. It all gives me a measure of where you are, and it tells me how much more potential there is.

Guh... SO MUCH potential!

Makes me just want to cut you into pieces and splatter you all over my walls.

That's romantic, right?

Machinery

I hover with my face just above his.

I can't trust myself to touch him in the moment because I want to crash into and through him with teeth and bone and blood and the hardness of clashing steel. And even though I am soft, really, all tender and smooth flesh that gives and bends, I am afraid that I will really hurt him.

I feel like I am snarling at him, breathing into his open mouth, watching his tongue tentatively reach out to survey the damage already done to him.

I'm not sure if I make any sound, but the animal noise is there in my throat and a thrumming is loud in my ears.

I hear a whining engine noise in my head, creaky brakes trying to slow a huge machine that wants to barrel over the top of everything in its way, giant cogs forging ahead under load, weighty and unstoppable. I bare my teeth and try to quell the aggression until it's manageable, under enough control that I can trust it.

He watches me, restrained, both flinching and wanting to reach for it, willing it to obliterate him.

I know if I wait long enough he will crane his neck to get to me, to invite me back in, and even as I nudge against him, I see him screw his eyes shut and try not to pull away when I shove myself into him again. It's like he forgets, in those moments of reprieve, how relieved he was when I stopped.

But he hates it when I stop.

List of Stories

Biting him 1
Meeting 5
Strip, boy 11
Raw 13
Good morning 15
Nightly spanking 21
Wash me..25
Kissing him 31
He waits 35
Putting him to bed 37
Card game..41
The couch...43
First time 45
Show me how to hurt you................53
Tethered 57
I feel like kissing.............................59
Breaking you 61
I love... 63
Crash...65

After the violence	69
Holding back	71
Kissing you awake	73
No rules	75
Offering	79
Things I am not doing to you	81
Coming when you are not coming	85
I know what you mean	87
This kiss	89
Convince me	91
Scent marking	93
Sex-noise	95
Best laid plans	97
Greedy slut	101
Sweet things	105
Men in kilts	107
Single minded passion	111
Your voice	115
Domme-space	117
Day 31 of chastity	119
Fun of hurting	121
Snippets	123
That is all	125
Tearing at your skin	127

Surrender 129
First meeting 131
Scared 133
It's okay 137
Gasping for breath 139
Rain hell 141
Stroking 143
Little Black Dress 145
Sweetness 147
Pornographic statue 149
Blather 151
More? 153
Slaps 155
Lick me 157
Saying 'no' 159
Kiss goodbye 161
Under instruction 163
Enough 165
Shy 167
Needles 169
She watched him 171
Airport 173
Button pushing 175
And then I come 177

Table boy	179
The tallness of being	181
Waiting	183
A bedtime story	187
Moments	191
Sweat	193
Wake up	195
Sleep kisses	197
Trust and fear	199
Collar	201
Prey	203
Petting	205
As always	207
"You hit me…"	209
Cutting to the core	211
Marking territory	213
Caning	215
Violence	219
Say…	221
Kissing noises	223
Arse show	227
Don't care	229
My cocks	231
He wears…	233

Buckling	235
Blur	237
The corner	239
Impact	241
Shoe shopping	243
Pieces of skin and bone	247
Good puppy	249
Please hurt me	251
Can I...?	253
Blindfold	255
I know...	257
Please	259
Second one nighter	261
My orgasm	263
Music festival	265
Drawing out hurt	269
Why chastity?	277
Yogacam	279
On kissing you	281
Public tease	285
Afterwards, kissing	289
Dirty secrets	291
There's something about him	295
Sexual violence	297

Face fuck 299

Rubbing myself raw......................303

Under his clothes...........................305

Another drink?..............................307

Boy under her heels......................311

Bedtime story.................................317

Good morning 319

Rope play 321

Introduction... 323

The proposition.............................325

Play list 327

An invitation 329

Water torture 331

Coming home 333

Here, boy..335

Kissing play parties......................339

Face touch 341

Fucking bitch.................................343

The first time 347

A day at work 353

Scary movie...................................355

Blow job 357

Order my lunch 361

Thinking about... 363

Kissing, is all 367

Beg me to be allowed to come 371

Dressing up 381

Pimping him out 387

Body canvas 389

Ask me to hurt you 393

The chair 399

When I get like this 403

Pegs 405

Thinking 411

Tears 415

I know you 417

Welcome home 425

Undressing 431

Aggression 435

Art and movies 437

Movie 439

Hurting 441

Because I can 443

Romance 445

Machinery 447

About the Author 457

About the Author

Sharyn Ferns is a dominant woman who is lucky enough to live at the beach in Australia with her imaginary cats and her laptop named Simon. She would like it noted that she has not named her other appliances, though she admits that her car is called Royal Highness and she is considering naming her beloved coffee machine 'Carl', though Carl is not at all sure about this.

She is passionate about submissive men, about writing, creative thinking, mindful living, and about seeing beauty in the world. She's a confirmed introvert despite the fact that she spews every intimate detail of her personal life out in public with verve and enthusiasm.

As a dominant, she is loving and selfish, affectionate and demanding, generous and uncompromising, deeply passionate and reserved. Complex and unique, like most people.

She writes a successful blog called Domme Chronicles where she has been throwing hotness and other random thoughts about her life and D/s relationships into the ether for the last five years. This is her first book.

She is known as 'Ferns' online, and you can connect with her at:

W: http://www.domme-chronicles.com

T: http://twitter.com/Ferns__ (double underscore!)

F: http://www.facebook.com/Ferns.DommeChronicles

E: ferns@domme-chronicles.com

Made in the USA
Middletown, DE
26 June 2017